Critical Acclaim for

'*My Friend Says It's B...*
Mrs Mortimer, bri...
unobtrusively skilful i...
and present crises in he...
– *Times Literary Supple...*

'Muriel Rowbridge do... ...reconciled" to the
pains of life, but she learns from them that the choice to
survive is worth making. She is, in fact, a true heroine'
– *Financial Times*

'Brilliant, if unnerving' – *Francis King*

'Miss Mortimer explores with suave virtuosity her
heroine's struggle towards self-realisation' – *Listener*

'An experienced and indeed much admired novelist'
– *The Bookman*

'One of our most outstanding contemporary novelists'
– *Spectator*

VIRAGO
MODERN
CLASSIC
NUMBER
319

Penelope Mortimer

was born in North Wales in 1918, the daughter of a vicar. She spent her childhood in Oxfordshire, a London suburb and Derbyshire, attending seven schools in all. At the age of seventeen she did a secretarial course and then went on to London University, which she was forced to leave a year later because of financial difficulties.

After four years of writing, her first novel, *Johanna* (1947), appeared. Since then Penelope Mortimer has produced eight other novels: *A Villa in Summer* (1954); *The Bright Prison* (1956); *Daddy's Gone-A-Hunting* (1958); *The Pumpkin Eater* (1962, an award-winning film, adapted for the screen by Harold Pinter); *My Friend Says It's Bullet-Proof* (1967); *The Home* (1971); *Long Distance* (1974) and *The Handyman* (1983, adapted by the author for a BBC film to be shown in 1989). Her autobiography, *About Time* (1979) was awarded the Whitbread Prize in 1980; her most recent publication, *Queen Elizabeth, A Life of the Queen Mother*, appeard in 1986. Since then she has written the screenplay for *A Summer Story* (1988), a film adaptation of John Galsworthy's short story, 'The Apple Tree'.

Though primarily a fiction writer, Penelope Mortimer has contributed regularly to *The New Yorker* and done a considerable amount of reviewing for both English and American newspapers and periodicals. She has also taught at the New School for Social Research in New York, and was for two years Visiting Professor to the Creative Writing Department at Boston University.

Penelope Mortimer has been married twice and has five daughters and one son. She lives in Gloucestershire where she is a keen gardener and visits London 'only when absolutely necessary'.

Published by VIRAGO PRESS Limited 1989,
20-23 Mandela Street, Camden Town, London NW1 0HQ.

First published in Great Britain by Hutchinson & Co. Ltd.
1967
Copyright © Penelope Mortimer 1967

British Library Cataloguing in Publication Data

Mortimer, Penelope
My friend says it's bullet-proof
I. Title
823'.914 [F]

ISBN 1-85381-008-80

Printed in Great Britain
by Cox and Wyman Ltd., Reading, Berks

PENELOPE MORTIMER

My Friend Says
It's Bullet-Proof

1

THE blonde stewardess was demonstrating the use of a life-jacket. She touched the lungs, the nipples of the jacket with delicate fingers, no more than indicating the nozzle and tapes. Her hands moved swiftly, lightly, through gestures which, in the real event, would be terrified and clumsy. The stewardess smiled all the time, her eyes were smiling as her fingers hovered, brushed against her yellow breasts.

Muriel Rowbridge folded back the cover of her notebook and wrote, on the first page: 'The stewardess is demonstrating the life-jacket . . .' She looked out of the window at the wet tarmac, a man in yellow oilskins waving his arms. She added, 'I'd sooner die,' because she felt, in a general way, that this was the truth. Death, under any circumstances, would be preferable to fear. The man sitting next to her glanced down at the notebook. She closed it, clipping the ball-point to the cover, which depicted some kind of oriental bird perched on a sprig of honeysuckle. The man registered her profile without looking at her, a trick he had learned thirty years ago as a provincial reporter—'Eyes in the back of your head, boy, that's the secret.' He saw a bony face with unkempt eye-

angelic to you, darling. The only woman, you'll have a ball. But do, well, join in, won't you? Don't go wandering off in one of your Virginia Woolf fits. Join in—you know? It'll do you a power of good, I promise.' Smile, salute, dismiss. Only yesterday, in the notebook she had left behind, she had written: 'General B's generosity and trust—frightening, which, of course, she means it to be. Join in, she says— therapy?'

So she hurried after them, her colleagues with their trousers beaten against their knees, plastic macs ballooning in the wind. But inside, in the great shedful of loot, she didn't recognise any of them. The counters were heaped with undesirable possessions, threats; she touched the spiky wool garments and felt her skin contract, sore as a bare knee on a doormat. Machinery, toys, whisky, cigars, musical boxes—what could she buy, to show willing? At last she chose a huge postcard of two Connemara ponies standing beside a well, and posted it to the son of her landlady, at boarding school in Sussex. He was eleven years old, and the only child she knew. The men joined her in the queue to re-board the aircraft. They held bottles in carrier bags, small parcels clutched to their chests among the cameras. They were pleased with themselves, thawing towards each other, throwing out remarks about wives, children, secretaries, which were immediately understood, as though they were giving a particular handshake or flicking back their lapels for identification. They had become a body, a group. She walked beside them like a woman walking beside a parade, hurrying to keep up. Back in the aircraft, the man

[9]

asked her whether Chanel No. 5 was suitable for an eighteen-year-old girl—he said he didn't know about such things. She said yes, she thought it was very suitable. He said, 'Are you sure you won't take your jacket off?' She unbuttoned it, allowed him to help her, allowed him to put it on the rack. Small, he thought, but not bad, not bad at all: perky.

*   *   *

The aircraft flew a straight course across the sky, the man offered her a drink, she had a vodka-and-tonic, he told her his name was Bill Anderson, that he worked for a Sunday newspaper, that he lived in Kent and the commuting was easy. She told him that her name was Muriel Rowbridge and she worked on a magazine which did not like to be thought of as a woman's magazine because its policy was that women were people like anyone else. At this he said, 'Ho, a feminist,' and she knew it would be useless to argue, so smiled with her eyes to show him what an absurdity this was. He offered her another drink, which she accepted, and after two meals he fell asleep, his mouth open and his head rigid, as though he were lying on his back in Farnborough. She took out the notebook and began to write, elbows pressed to her sides:

'When I sat alone in that place and thought, I began to feel the most extraordinary sensation of fear and emptiness. Then I tried to shock myself, imagining horrors, but it wasn't any use. The whole history of the Jewish race left me cold. Starving children, war, dismemberment, injustice—was that all? My mouth hung open, the breath went in and out; my tongue, the insides of my cheeks, were soft and moist. A draught coming from under the door caught me by the heels, like two cold hands. I imagined, briefly, that I was held down in my chair by spectral hands, by my own shadow. If you had come into the room scourged, mutilated, I would have looked at you lacklustre thinking, that's the human condition.

'This is the only thing that shocks me any more: my own deformity. When I encourage myself to a certain pitch of self-disgust the whole fantasy disintegrates as softly as burning paper, and there I am, back again, equipped with pity, intelligence, even humour of a kind. The vacant expression on my face changes, I become alert, decide to change an electric plug, pay a bill, do some work, make a telephone call. I tell myself that compassion and love are a matter of habit: to behave well is to be well, one can control fear by not allowing it to be felt. I don't believe a word of it, of course, but one has to survive. A sense of outrage isn't enough.

'One way of scaring oneself stiff is to imagine looking into a mirror and finding no reflection. I think of the people I know, and look in them for my own reflection, it isn't there. They may be looking in me for theirs—how can I tell? Here is another fantasy: a world populated by mirrors with little running feet, smacking up against each other in the street, cold as ice-blocks, every impact seven years' bad luck. Two mirrors reflecting each other reflect nothing; and yet of course they do; they reflect each other. And so on.

'What I needed was some contact with reality—

sitting up there all day like a frozen bird, feathers
bunched, head drawn in, anaesthetised with loneliness.
I used to look down into the street, peering craftily
between the chintz curtains: through the window I
saw the dirty bookshop, the sex cinema, the Wine
Store, the cut-price refrigerators growing mouldy out
on the pavement, their orange price tags cut and cut
again. If I watched for ten minutes there wasn't one
man who didn't hesitate outside the cinema. Some
walked on, as though the fault had been only momentary, their movement afterwards even more rapid and
purposeful; others, absorbed, shifted sideways from
photograph to photograph, they wore scarves but
no gloves, their hands deep in their pockets. They
stood in this at-ease position long enough to digest
one picture, then, drawing their right feet up to their
left, pausing for a moment for reflection, they moved
the left foot again, slumped, clamped their eyes to
the next nipple . . . I envied their simplicity, did I,
their lack of shame? I began to envy people who
believed in God. No, I envied people who could
accept that such things are meaningless. No, that's
not it. I simply envied.

'I'm afraid of people who talk. I, simply, unlike
St. Sebastian stuck with arrows, envy. Sebastian says:
It's all right, I'm merely stuck with arrows, that is
my condition, I'm quite used to it. I have never seen
a rebellious Christ, tearing at the nails, spitting out
the vinegar, throwing his head from side to side
rejecting death. He went through all that in Gethse-
mane, they say. How do we know he did? He didn't
try to escape, did he? It doesn't matter. We try to

escape. Not far away from my room, just to the left of a skyscraper, they told me there was a house where elderly men could be crucified in comfort at considerable expense.

'I used to walk round my room, pretending it was a long journey round the estate. I was creeping with a blind man along the herbaceous border, deceiving him with every flower. The dahlias are fine this year; yes, the roses make a good show; we must bed and divide, pot, prune, seed, touch the catalogues. In fact I knew that there was nothing but groundsel, chickweed and thistles; the dead michaelmas daisies were so dry that one thought he could hear them rattling. What if it had been the other way round—his belief unshakable that the mown grass and fertilised soil, the cultivation we told him about, was really a rubbish-dump, bomb-site, the flourishing gladioli becoming willow herb between his prying fingers? Well, there was no way of proving anything to him. I was cheating him all along, by growing, making awful faces, squatting down before his blind eyes to relieve myself, or worse. Saturated in isolation, having lost all deference to myself, I thought of showing a garden to a blind man, of posturing in front of him because he could not see; of keeping away from his groping hands because touch, of all things, is the most dangerous.

'I didn't know who I was—man or woman, young or old. When they let me get dressed, I wore camel-hair trousers, a soft sweater from the men's boutique across the road, suède boots rather grimy on the instep. Like all games, this wore very thin. I was

[13]

exhausted by the time I reached the doorway, the corridor outside; merely plodding along, one foot after another, revolted by the whole business. The temptation to indulge myself was overwhelming. I hunched my shoulders, flicking my eyes from side to side, knowing they sparkled. I said out loud, in a gnome's voice, "I'm two for the price of one, you know. Two for the price of one." The telephone breathed deeply, deeply sleeping in a patch of sunlight. A click, and the long, majestic diapason of the refrigerator in the nurses' kitchen, freezing itself to death.

'The only true contact with reality is being joined with another body; then you are lost, free, alone at last. The navel and fontanel close in infancy, shutting off natural supplies of thought and feeling. What are you meant to do? You might say it's easier for women —the umbilical cord is threaded straight through them, mother on one end, child on the other. Women are what you might call a means of communication. But men, what about men? Sliced off, tied up, sewn up, sealed, their only remaining apertures intended for giving out some inexhaustible supply of good or evil. I used to hesitate at the doorway, turned myself to stone, fingers delicately extended, eyeballs gritty, sex, buttocks, knuckles marble, no entrance anywhere. A balloon out of my stiff lips: "I'm two for the price of one, known in some circles as bedtime Charlie". It wasn't convincing. One shot of methydrene, I'm told, and you can convince anyone of this sort of rubbish, even yourself. . . .'

The plane lurched, the 'f' scrawled across the page.

'Ladies and gentlemen, will you make sure your seat-belts are fastened while we're going through this turbulence.' Bill Anderson woke wildly, grabbing the arms of his seat. 'Where are we?' he asked, meaning, 'Where am I?'

Muriel closed the notebook. 'We're flying at thirty-one thousand feet and will be over the northern tip of Newfoundland in thirty minutes.'

'That's what they said?'

'That's what they said.'

'You've been writing all this time? Writing away?'

'Just notes,' she said cautiously. 'Homework.'

'My God!' he said.

2

ARRIVAL was orderly, they were met by a Public
Relations man who carried her suitcase, she felt
singled out but relieved; they were carried on a long
moving pathway towards the outside world, the
Public Relations man told her many statistics about
the length and weight and cost of this pathway, the
construction of the airport, the amount of internal
and external passengers who passed through it each
year; she listened attentively. She had never been out
of Europe before, General Bird's descriptions had
been confined to the pace, the rarefied air and the
strength of the martinis.

'You have friends here?' the Public Relations man
asked. 'Relatives?'

'No.'

'Eighty-five per cent of our visitors from England,'
he said, 'have relatives here somewhere.'

'Well . . . my grandfather came from South Africa.'

'Ah,' he said. 'Then that explains it.' He helped her
into the bus, the party of men followed; as they
passed her seat some of them smiled quickly,
acknowledging her presence for the first time. She
thought she would never get to know them; that

she would return home as secretive, as isolated, as she was now.

*   *   *

Tropical heat in the hotel bedroom: she flung open the window and leant over the boiling grid to take great gulps of warm air. It was five o'clock, the rush hour, traffic crawling round the square, police cars flashing and howling to some rescue or arrest. At home it would be ten o'clock at night, her bedtime for the past few months. She imagined the flat empty, the ivies dying, dust already glazing the top of the television set, the dressing-table with its mirror swivelled round to show the varnished wood backing and the price tag from Camden Passage, where she had bought it in the spring. Forty-five shillings it had cost, a bit mildewed, but adequate. 'Ramsey peers into the mirror and finds himself pockmarked, for a moment he really believes he's diseased. Then he promises me another mirror, and today it arrived, a great thing in a gilt frame like another room for two other people to make love in. But when we stood in front of it we were bulbous, our legs like little growths; though we laughed, it was really appalling. R was Lautrec naked . . .'

She came back into the room, leaving the window open. At 6.30 they were to meet in the foyer of the hotel to be taken by bus to what was called, in their itinerary, a reception. She unpacked slowly, pondering on the reception, imagining the men shaving, drinking their whisky, unpinning clean shirts and dropping the pins in ashtrays out of habitual thrift. At first she had been entirely concerned with the thought, the prospect of death. Then they told her she was not going to die and her concern changed to a sense of outrage; she became convinced that no one could ever feel anything for her, sexually, but pity and disgust. She sent Ramsey away, his mirror after him. They said she would get over this too, and suggested therapy. But she did not want to get over it, the cheat she was perpetrating on the world by pretending to be a normal woman gave her a kind of terrible liveliness; without that liveliness, that feeling of perpetual shock, she believed that she would drift into an apathy which would be worse than death. She went back to work in new clothes, everything hidden. They called her brave behind her back, but treated her, according to the General's directions, with affectionate indifference. Very few people telephoned her at home, or asked her out, in case she should feel pitied or find it difficult to refuse. The men who had previously patted or stroked her, out of friendliness, avoided her; the women, in her presence, avoided the men, obscurely ashamed of themselves. At one time she had written a beauty column, imploring readers to moisten their skins and have contemporary eyes; now they gave her what the General called a free hand, to write what she liked. The notebooks became more confused: 'Savoy, 6.15 . . . Hurricane belt, average winter temp 72, but heavy rainfall, the Biminis—Bond? . . . My kind of fear is not organic; it creeps into exposed places and lodges there, it infects little by little, it colours the bone as it eats it.

Occasioned by continual sense of danger—very personal, so deep, private and inaccessible to reason that no amount of jollying-up, pepping, brisking or resorting to rum in the tea can reach it. Persecution re unions & strikes. Need for competition, I.C.I., Courtaulds. I was never afraid of death and for many years I wasn't afraid of pain. God tempers the wind, said Maria, to the shorn lamb, 4000 in care (London) for homelessness, 7000 indirectly resulting.'

She had a bath, fitted her cold undetectable breast into a clean brassière, stood her hand-mirror on the window-sill and made up her eyes with care, leaving the rest of her face empty. Seven thousand what? Indirectly resulting from what? Now the job was important: she must concentrate more, care more. For nearly three years she had taken it for granted that some day, some year, when his divorce was through and it seemed suitable, she would marry Ramsey; she would have children, and when they were old enough she would go back to work. Now she saw this plan as a series of clichés without one positive feeling to bring it to life, without a single query. Why would she have married Ramsey, of all people; why would she have had children? She couldn't remember. If she did well on this trip, keeping to facts and not wandering off in one of her Virginia Woolf fits, she could start thinking about promotion. In the end (what end, when?) she could be wearing a grey silk battle tunic with rhinestone buttons. She opened the notebook, where the f had scrawled across the page: 'One shot of methydrene, I'm told, and you can convince anyone of this sort of rubbish, even yourself . . .' Not even accurate. She sat down at the desk, half dressed, and started a new page. 'There is something different about travel in this State. This State is big. It has about 250,000 lakes and 140 million acres of forest land, 83,000 miles of road link it all together . . .'

*   *   *

Bill Anderson was the first to arrive in the foyer. He was disconsolate. The cold water didn't work in his shower, he'd forgotten the adaptor for his electric razor, the barber's was shut, bloody awful country. He watched Muriel coming down the stairs; she went to the bookstall, put on a pair of black horn-rimmed glasses and began to turn the postcard rack round slowly, but without choosing a card. Smashing legs, nice gear, good figure—not his cup of char, though, didn't turn him on one bit. When she came up to him he was standing with his back to her, staring out through the revolving door, shaking a Camel out of the pack.

'Want one?'

'No, thanks.'

'You don't?'

'I used to.'

'Gave it up?'

'Yes. That's right.'

'I don't even try. Might as well die of that as anything else. Comfortable, are you? Room all right?'

'Oh, yes. It looks over the square. Terribly hot, though.'

'Terribly hot. Yes.'

'How's your room?'

'I've had worse. No cold water in the shower, but you can't expect everything, they're all bloody inefficient.'

'But I thought . . .'

'A hundred years behind the times. Look at the department stores, I've seen better in Wigan. They haven't seen a mini-skirt for forty years. You'll cause quite a stir in that, Miss Rowbridge.'

'I hope . . .'

'Very nice too, if I might say so. Good pair of legs, might as well show 'em. Goes for everything else too, of course.'

The others began to gather, looking more refreshed than Anderson. She stood alone, thinking that this was how it would be at the reception, at all the receptions, wondering if she could bear it. No one she knew had ever heard her cry for help; only a nurse, once, in the lofty hospital room. ' . . . I sat in Fortnum & Mason's Soda Counter and observed Flora's face as closely and minutely as I might observe my own in a mirror. A round, ruthless pudding; a crystallised fruit. She told me some story about her mother's pig, how her mother tried to sell the pig, which was pregnant, and the pig had its litter in a bush on the way to market. This, Flora said, was a deeply moving story, and so I suppose it is. I was soundlessly yelling among the cream cakes, Help me, help me. But I listened about the pig and walked off in the slight rain after friendly kisses and promises of going to Spain, Switzerland, the Hebrides together, anything to relieve her lot. . . .'

Flora, the wife of Ramsey, a female Cronus stuffing little people into her mouth; crunch and swallow and down they went, the bulges showing. Oh, don't let's be beastly to Flora, who loved as well as hated her husband's mistress; and the hate was solely because she was indigestible, the mistress, Muriel, myself. Compassion must come before long, surely: acceptance, understanding, compassion. In the meanwhile, are all these men husbands? What a strange race, so unavailable, loyal and full of resentment, like priests trying to mingle, trying to compromise with everything they most detest.

'Do you feel better now?' The man wore a crumpled suit and the smile, like hers, of a shy person trying to be sociable.

'Better?'

'Well. I mean. Rested and so on.'

'Oh. Yes, thank you. Are we going? Won't we be late?'

'We seem to be going.'

The Public Relations man was shepherding them out of the revolving doors. The crumpled man walked beside her. 'My name's Godfrey Wrench. With a W. You are . . .?'

'Muriel Rowbridge.'

'You're here for a paper?'

'A magazine.'

'You've been here before?'

'Never. Have you?'

'Never been out of Europe—oh, except North Africa, in the war.'

They climbed into the bus. He sat beside her.

'There's a Henry Moore in the square,' he said.

'Really?'

'Mm. "Reclining Woman". What do you do on the magazine?'

'I . . . have a column, a sort of general column. What do you do?'

'Oh, odds and sods, bits and pieces. Books really.'

'You're a reviewer?'

'Sometimes. No, I mean write them.'

'Would I know . . . ?'

'You wouldn't have read any. Theology.'

'But you're a journalist?'

'That's right,' he said dourly. He had a very clean face, a forty-year-old schoolboy, scoured, almost beardless, innocent.

She asked, 'Are you married?'

He nodded, offering her a cigarette; she felt he approved her refusal.

'Any children?'

'Three.'

'Well,' she said, 'that's something.' She didn't mean that it was an achievement, but that it was at least something. To have children, she imagined, was to see into the future; to populate the distance with grown men and women with functioning memories, of which one would always be a part. In the latter part of the century only one middle-aged man might remember her—a woman who sent a postcard of ponies from Ireland. This was a considerable relief to her now; she was not sure how it might seem in ten years' time.

He glanced down at her hands. 'Are you married?'

[23]

'No.'

Why not, he was asking. She said, 'I was . . . engaged for a long time. It broke up.'

'Recently?'

'Well . . . about five months ago.'

'I'm sorry.'

'There's no need to be, honestly.'

'You mean you're happier as you are?'

'No . . . it's quite different. I don't suppose we would ever have got married, really.'

'Why not?'

'There were complications. You know. Anyway, I don't think I understand marriage.'

'The whole thing's a matter of habit, really, love included. Habit and territory.'

'Territory?'

'Yes. Establishing your claim to territory. Hanging on.'

She said, 'I never thought about territory.'

He grunted, unable or unwilling to explain further. The bus pulled up in a side street. Godfrey Wrench and Muriel were the first to get out. He did not help her down the steps. The others joined them on the pavement, saying how exhausted they were, how much they needed a drink. They filed into the house, which was small and hot and brightly lit, with a cocktail-party sound coming from upstairs. Muriel kept close to Wrench. She said, 'Don't desert me.' He smiled and said, 'I won't.' They went up the stairs and were met by their host, an art director, who immediately took her away from Wrench and introduced her to a group of women—well-dressed, accurately made-up professional women who could tell her what she ought to want to know. After half of her gin-and-tonic she began to feel that she had lived for a week without sleep; when it was finished she no longer heard what the women were saying, but watched them in stony amazement as their mouths moved, their skin folded up and spread out again, their heads proudly carried and waving, like so many sea anemones. She looked about for Wrench, but couldn't see him. Bill Anderson was standing un-naturally still, looking at his third bourbon. When she reached him, she asked, 'Have you seen Mr. Wrench, Godfrey Wrench?'

He said, 'I told you what would happen. They've never seen . . . anything like it. Cods' eyes.'

'Have you seen Mr. Wrench, Godfrey Wrench?'

'Fish eyes. Only decently dressed woman in the room. Did I say decently?' He gave a humourless bark, immediately stifled.

She wandered into the next room, but Wrench wasn't there. She knew very well that he had escaped, was walking back to the hotel already. She sat down, holding her empty glass on her knees.

Someone said, 'You aren't drinking.'

She shook her head, nauseated.

'You don't want to?'

She shook her head again. The man sat down beside her. He was wearing a brown pin-striped suit and a waistcoat. She narrowed her eyes, trying to focus.

'I'm tired,' she said.

'They shouldn't bring you here, when you've just arrived.'

[25]

'And my vaccination hurts.'

'Where?'

She vaguely indicated her left thigh. 'I had a bath.'

'You shouldn't have got it wet, you know.'

'That's what I mean. Are you a journalist?'

'No. No, I live here.'

As though it were an occupation. She closed her eyes for a moment. When her eyes were shut she felt him take away the glass. He asked, 'Have you eaten? You should eat something.'

She said nothing. She felt, heard, that he had gone away. When she opened her eyes the art director was coming rapidly towards her, she had the impression that he wouldn't be able to stop, and pressed herself against the back of the sofa, steadying herself. But he drew up with his trousers against her legs, the toes of his shoes between her feet. 'Miss Rowbridge, we must feed you hungry people. I hope you will accompany us to dinner?'

'Now?'

'Right now.' He glowed, encouraging her.

'Thank you.'

'Robert will take you. He has your coat. We will follow before long.'

The art director's phrases decorated the sympathy he felt for her, it seemed she should curtsey and move into a quadrille; it was hard enough to stand upright and allow Robert, the man in the brown suit, to hang her coat round her shoulders. He took her right arm; she moved behind him so that he should take her left arm. They walked with dignity towards the stairs.

She said, 'I'm not really plastered, you know.'

[26]

'Of course not. Just tired and hungry,' he said. 'And the vaccination.'

*   *   *

He guided her into a thirty-year-old Bentley, a silver hearse with a glass partition between the back and front seats, a speaking tube and a small vase above the dashboard containing two carnations and a sprig of maidenhair. She thought he must be some kind of caterer. As they drove, he sang from time to time, a few bars of no recognisable tune. There was no conversation. When they arrived at the restaurant the head waiter was deferential; they installed her next to a huge open fire and gave her a bowl of soup, as though she were suffering from exposure. Robert sat opposite her, watching the spoon travel steadily from the plate to her mouth, doing her good. She was not used to so much attention. She had come to overlook ordinary kindness because she was so directed inwards, desperately searching for independence and self-sufficiency. This necessity not to be loved must always have been part of her, growing perhaps out of self-protection, defending herself against a blind father who could only be moved by speech or touch. Masochistic, Ramsey had called her, now wishing he had bitten off his tongue, no doubt. But endurance of pains—disappointment, loneliness, frustration, confusion of all sorts—could have another motive—to build insensitivity, at least a working substitute for strength. She had indeed sent Ramsey away, his mirror after him; not in order to enjoy her suffering, but in an effort to contend with less of it. Sitting in this strange restaurant, city, country, continent, drunk, gulping soup, aware of the tender observation of the man Robert, she felt literally reborn, with no past, no predictable personality, no image to which she must conform.

'How's the vaccination?'

She picked up her soup bowl, drinking the dregs. 'I suppose it needs a dry plaster.'

'We will get you some.' The royal 'we', or did he have a wife at home, a medicine cupboard?

'Do you call it plaster?'

'Band-Aid, probably. Plaster we put on walls.'

'You're from Europe, aren't you?'

'Hungary. I left in 1956. You are English?'

'Well. My grandfather came from South Africa. Yes.'

'Your mother?'

'Welsh.'

'So you are not English at all?'

She laughed. 'Yes, I'm English. I mean, there's no such thing, really, is there? My grandmother was all right. She was a Cornish Jew.'

His eyes closed a little. 'You aren't serious.'

'Yes, I am. She was a result of the Armada, a beautiful Spanish Jew shipwrecked off Land's End. It might have been Torquay, doesn't matter. She had an enormous nose and she was very dark except for her hair, which was absolutely white, and she washed it in soda-water every day.'

'I do not find it funny, to be Jewish.'

She retracted quickly. 'I never said it was funny. I

simply said she washed her hair in soda-water. My grandmother. Not because she was Jewish—because she was my grandmother. Oh, my God!'

When she raised her face from her hands, where she had been smothering laughter, he was smiling at her, his eyes alert and gleaming. She put out her hand suddenly. 'Thank you for looking after me. I thought I was going to die in that place.'

He took her hand. 'I thought you were going to die in that place.'

The cocktail party arrived. Bill Anderson sat down at another table with the wives, two girls with shiny brown faces and good teeth raced each other for the chairs next to Robert, arrived panting and laughing as though the music had stopped. He introduced them to Muriel; their names were Rowan and Pat and they said 'Hi!' simultaneously, grinning at her frankly, without suspicion. The art director asked if he might be permitted to sit with her, then talked steadily and quietly about art in the city, their great young painter, Shimon Richler, his murals for the new Civic Centre Complex, the number of art galleries opened in the last year, the increasing popularity of art schools as opposed to technical colleges. It was like being massaged with words, the back of her neck, her spine, the tense thigh muscles relaxed, her eyelids seemed to swell until they were blocking her eyes, she was falling asleep.

'You want to go?' Robert asked.

'But you haven't eaten.'

'I'm not hungry.'

'You should get a good night's rest,' the art director

said. 'If Robert will accompany you back to the hotel . . .'

'Thank you. I'm . . . it's silly, I'm dropping.' She stood up, the eager polished faces of Rowan and Pat shone like suns, their features only vaguely perceptible; she felt no guilt about not joining in with the journalists as Robert again guided her away. The Public Relations man came hurrying after them.

'Tomorrow we go to the mountains, to see the autumn colouring. You have never seen anything like the autumn colouring, Miss Rowbridge. We meet in the foyer at 11 a.m. You will enjoy this, I know.'

'Of course,' she said.

'Good. Then sleep soundly.'

In the Bentley she stretched out as though on a sofa. They stopped outside a drugstore and Robert got out, came back with a packet of Band-Aids which, without a word, he dropped in her lap. Two taxis were straddled across the street, the drivers shouting at each other. Robert switched off the engine, patiently waiting; looking down through the windscreen was like sitting in the Royal Box, seeing a mime performed on a distant stage. One of the taxi-drivers, young, with a shaven head and a tartan windcheater, got out, approached the other taxi and began to kick it silently. The other driver waited, as though respecting this ceremony. The young one was wearing sneakers, he did no damage. When he had expressed his rage he got back into his own taxi and drove away. The other driver shrugged his shoulders, spread his arms, got into his cab and drove off in the opposite direction.

Without comment, Robert started the engine again; they continued their dignified progress through the empty streets.

He switched on the radio. 'What is it?' he asked.

'I don't know . . . Brahms?'

'Could be Liszt.'

'No, it's not Liszt . . . Schubert?'

'I don't think it's Schubert.'

They stopped outside the hotel. Like a child after a party, she gathered herself together, prepared to thank him very much, held out her hand. He briefly kissed the back of the strong, rigid hand, said good night.

She asked, 'Shall I see you again?'

'Of course. Sometime, somewhere.' The vagueness of a man to whom people are always accessible.

'Well, then. Good night.'

She climbed out of the car and hurried up the hotel steps. The porter looked at her curiously as she took the key; upstairs, she discovered that her eyes drooped out of great black rings in a white face. She glanced at the notebook on the table, opened it on eighty-three thousand miles of roadway, closed it again, thankfully too tired to write. In two movements she peeled off her clothes, then fell into bed and turned off the light, falling asleep immediately, almost before she was aware that it was dark.

During the night—in fact, it was only half an hour later—her telephone rang. She thought she was at home, that it was Ramsey, that she was frightened. She groped for the receiver. Without announcing himself, a voice said, 'Chopin.'

[31]

'Chopin?'

'Good night. Sleep well.'

A click, silence. She lay on her back, her right arm behind her head, and went to sleep again easily.

3

WHEN she woke up, it was early; she put on her nightdress and wrap and leaned out of the window to watch the square. The metal flag-pole outside the hotel was red-hot in the sun; everything seemed on fire, great slabs of grey and gold in the sky. A howling scarlet car shot down the empty street. Church bells began ringing towards eight o'clock; the few trees in the plaza glowed fervently against the blackened stone of the City Hall; the air was clean and cool, the streets washed, the few people neither hurried nor loitered, they looked as though they had slept well and enjoyed Sundays.

She took the notebook and ball-point back to bed, ordered a lavish breakfast, lay on her stomach in the sun: 'The city, 1,395,400, 76% Catholic, 300 years old. Now I've been out of bed to look at it I see a dozen green and purple spots dancing over the page, more with the left eye than the right. Would rather spend the day here than with the autumn colouring. Developers of the new Civic Centre Complex inviting artists to compete for over 20,000 dollars in commissions for interior theme of Modern Art Museum. Robert who? Somebody who sees an inch of me sticking out of the ground, and digs, may of course be digging for buried treasure, or an unexploded bomb, or just a bit of shapeless junk. In the same way I don't know that once I'm discovered, dug out and exposed to the ordinary human air, they won't turn away in disgust from what they've found—useless, a waste of time. Couldn't take the risk. What risk? Two thousand six hundred and seventy miles from Liverpool, what risk?'

The breakfast arrived, orange juice packed in ice, eggs sunny side up, a decanter of coffee, a load of newspaper that disgorged little newspapers like a Russian doll. She thanked the waiter, who said she was welcome and gave an appalled look at the open window. Tucked up now, the bedclothes under her armpits, she smiled at him about the heating, the English, the English passion for fresh air and pneumonia. When he had gone, she luxuriously ate the breakfast and read the women's supplement, reminding herself that this was her job. 'Life in the 1960s offers exceptional opportunities to the female of the species and as she crosses new thresholds she expresses her delight by choosing clothes that fit into the scene around a boardroom table, do her honour at functions connected with her professional or social activities. She welcomes new fabrics, colours and stylings that enhance her good points, refuses to let a preoccupation with youth stand in the way of material advancement since she's discovered how to be chic, vital and attractive in a newly conservative way . . . Hair styling is designed to raise the wearer's centre of gravity, jewellery to evoke the delicacy and magic of an

Arabian night . . .' She wondered, grinning to herself, whether to send this on a giant postcard to the General; but then realised, abruptly and for the first time, that her relationship with the General did not include jokes, and that her own side of it was in fact based on fear, dislike, even contempt. How could she be contemptuous of the General, that woman's woman with her convex silver fingernails, her thin legs with little bumps on the shins (A sign of age, surely? Young women had smooth shins), her passion for what she called the elegant and *outré*, her sympathy with the under-privileged, her connections, her ability? How dared she be contemptuous of anyone, let alone the ladies crossing the threshold to their boardroom table? Muriel Rowbridge, what's going to become of you? What can you do instead? Farm, garden, pot, paint, run a pineapple plantation, teach, work in a pet store, write a great novel? She shot out her legs, sending the newspapers cascading to the floor: bath, dress, organise, pull yourself together, prepare for the journalists . . . The telephone rang, she looked at it in surprise for a moment.

'Yes?'

'Good morning. Did you sleep well?'

'Oh. Oh, yes. Thank you.'

'You had breakfast already?'

'Yes. Yes, I did.'

'A large breakfast?'

'Enormous.'

'Very well. I have to go and take my boat in. It is about eighty miles from here. Do you want to come?'

'Your boat?'

'A small sailing dinghy. We have to pack it in for the winter.'

'But I have to see the autumn colouring.'

'You'll see that as well, I promise you. In fact, it is impossible to avoid.'

'When are you leaving?'

'In half an hour. I will wait for you outside the hotel.'

'I have to be back this evening.' She leaned across the bed, groping for the itinerary. 'It's another reception, the musical director, I have to be back by five-thirty.'

'You'll be back.'

'Did you . . . say Chopin?'

'Chopin, yes. See you in half an hour. Wear trousers.'

She rang down to Reception, asked for Geoffrey Wrench's room number. He answered as soon as she rang, as though the telephone were part of his hand and didn't have to be reached for.

'Look,' she said, 'I've been asked to go to the country for the day. I don't know who I should tell. Would you be very kind and say . . . well, I'll be back for the party this evening?'

'Of course. I do apologise for deserting you last night, but you seemed O.K. and I was knocked out. Sorry you won't be with us today, though.'

'Yes. Yes, I'm sorry too.' 'Liar,' she said to herself out loud. She scooped up armfuls of newspaper, there was no waste-basket, so she pushed the lot into a drawer. Away with you, board-women bored

[36]

women bawd women. There was only one pause in the speed of her dressing; a few moments while she stood with the horny, fluid-filled breast dangling from her hand, defeated by the thought of the possibilities, the improbabilities, the obscene cheat of being a female impersonator. TREAT YOUR BREAST-FORM EXACTLY AS YOU TREAT YOUR OWN BREAST. Never place on or near a radiator. DO NOT pin or pierce with pins. Do not be shot by arrows, for the fluid will drain through the drainage tubes and you will be left with a breast like an old toy, the stopper lost summers ago. Remember the jokes: 'They make them of birdseed, I believe. Imagine going to Trafalgar Square'; and just before the pentothal sent her swinging, she had seen very clearly Napoleon, his left hand plunged inside his greatcoat: 'I feel a right tit,' and had gone into it giggling drunk. Well. Never mind. Don't think about it, habit makes perfect. And once she was blurred in a man's cashmere sweater, trousered and booted, the swagger and liveliness returned. She brushed her hair with long strokes, as she had learned to do to exercise her muscles, whistling breathily as though grooming herself; and left her eyes undressed, like child's eyes, with the brief thought that this plainness might help to discourage any idea of availability and willingness. She stuffed the notebook and pen into her handbag, folded her nightdress, tidied up last night's clothes. It was precisely half an hour since he had telephoned. She closed the window, out of some obscure wish to be considerate, and left the room, walking slowly along the corridor, avoiding the lift, walking down the stairs

[37]

and through the lobby in order to be a few minutes
late.

*   *   *

The Bentley was not outside the hotel; she felt a
twinge of disappointment, expecting him to be
reliable and punctual, this man who bought Band-Aid
and owned a boat. The square was dazzling, the light
so bright and clear that it hit the eyes like spring
water. She walked down on to the pavement, he
opened the door of a dark green sports car, and
leaning out, said, 'Good morning.' For a moment
she didn't recognise him, and began to walk
away.

'But it's a different car.'

'You object? We can fetch the Bentley.'

'Of course not.' But she felt oddly annoyed as she
climbed into the car, bent double as though creeping
into a Wendy house.

'What is it, anyway?'

'A Ferrari.'

'I don't know much about cars. I mean, only
obvious ones.'

'You drive?'

'Yes, but there's not much point in London—the
traffic.'

'You have a car?'

'We—I did have, until recently.'

'I have a Triumph in the country. An old one.'

She felt a positive resentment against his three cars,
his correct country clothing; this resentment was

disappointing. He sang occasionally, as he had done last night, and did not talk much, except to answer her polite questions. He was a company lawyer, presumably successful, unmarried. He sat very straight in the low seat and drove with the same decorum that he had driven the Bentley. He was very thin, almost skeletal, and very neat; she thought he must be about forty.

When they got out of the city, a great network of freeways and flyovers led in every direction over the flat, boggy land. They crawled along as though the car were sleeping and he did not want to disturb it. She smiled, to disguise her irritation.

'Do you always drive so slowly?'

'There is a speed limit. The fines are severe.'

'It seems a pity. I mean, with a car like this.'

'I don't let her go,' he said. 'I hold her.'

'Why do you have three cars, anyway?'

He thought for a moment, then shrugged his shoulders. 'I don't know. How many pairs of stockings do you have at the moment?'

'I don't know.'

'Handkerchiefs?'

'I don't know.'

'Lipsticks?'

'Three.'

'Only three?'

'But that isn't the same, is it?'

He turned, looked at her, smiled. 'Why not?'

She stayed silent. The autumn colouring had certainly begun, but out of some childish refusal to appear impressed she did not comment on it.

After a while he asked, 'Well?'

'Well?'

He indicated the woods blazing with all the colours of fire—purple, indigo, scarlet, coral, jets of luminous gold. 'Your colouring.'

'I know. It's fantastic.'

'It happens every year.'

She could not tell whether he found this fact miraculous or tedious. His habit of ending a conversation before it had begun made her uneasy.

'You're nervous,' he said.

She lied. 'No.'

He tilted the driving mirror a little, and she realised that this was in order that he could watch her without turning his head. Their eyes met for a moment in the mirror, flicked away again.

He asked gently, 'What's the matter?'

'Nothing. Really. Nothing.'

He sang for a moment, and let the matter drop. After a mile or so he readjusted the mirror. His hand, loosely cupped over the gear lever, lay against her leg.

She looked everywhere, trying to see, to contain, everything: many notices, fifty dollar fine for litter droppers, Picnic Area Ahead (always ahead, never here); Antiques, Antiquities for sale, black and white cows, timber houses with porches for sitting on, stone colonial houses with lawns stretching down to the road and letter boxes on stakes, villages pillaged with the coral and fire trees, a few horses, no people but the old, expressionless, fat, Sunday people driving their huge cars, an occasional child hanging limp over

[40]

the back seat; swings in every other garden, cars parked haphazard round the houses like toys left out for the night; Motels, Cabins to let, now and then a lake, possibly always the same lake, the water whipped metal, straddled sometimes by flimsy bridges.

'Do you come here every weekend?'

'In the summer, yes. Do you sail?'

'No. No, I don't.'

'But you swim?'

She lied again, without thinking. 'No.' She was in fact a good swimmer, but suddenly alarmed that he might suggest stopping at some heated pool, hiring costumes, drinking martinis by steaming green water. Such a thing had never happened to her in her life, and she had no idea why the danger of it seemed so probable. They were complete strangers, completely unpredictable to each other, their conversation so far confined to nationality, cars, and what she considered to be wealthy forms of sport: probably he would ask her in a minute whether she rode, water-skied, where she spent the winter. She wanted to surprise or shock him, but could think of nothing to say.

'How far is it—the place where you keep your boat?'

'The weather isn't good, it'll be too choppy to bring her in. We will have lunch and go back.'

All right, he's as bored as I am. People can't come together suddenly, without preparation, and understand.

'Ta-rum, ta-rum, ta-rum,' he sang, looking straight ahead.

Not caring any longer, she took out the notebook

and ball-point and wrote, in the steady car: 'He sang these few bars like a bus blows its horn round Mediterranean corners, for warning, self-protection and the hell of it.'

'What are you writing?'

'Nothing. I'm a journalist. If I don't make notes, I forget.'

'What will you write about?'

'Oh . . . you know. Women. How they live, what they wear, that kind of thing.'

'And men?'

'I don't have to write about men.'

'You make such a clear distinction?'

'I don't. My magazine does.'

'And you write . . . only for your magazine?'

'Yes.'

'It sounds impertinent, perhaps, but I don't believe you.'

'What do you think, then?'

He shrugged again. 'How should I know?'

You could, if you gave me the chance to tell you. We're quarrelling, and it's absurd. As though to contradict her, to compensate for the indifference of his shrugged shoulders, he smiled at her with great sweetness and momentarily touched the back of her neck with the back of his gloved hand.

'Hungry?'

Again she lied, overdoing it: 'Ravenous.' But they couldn't drive on like this, through nowhere, to nowhere, pointlessly.

('The blind father is taken for Sunday outings, the daughter goes with him as guide, Mama drives

wearing a round felt hat, maroon coloured, with
a small feather in the hat band, it comes from
Henry Heath. There is a haystack, a man pushing a
pram.

  ' "No, dear. It was not a man."

  ' "Yes, it was".

  ' "No, dear. It was a young woman. In trousers."

  ' "It was the father, pushing the pram."

  ' "Muriel, how can you? Reggie, don't believe
her!"

  ' "I don't mind," the father says, "whether it was
a man or a woman. Shall we say, a person pushing
a pram? Continue, Muriel."

  'She tells the truth. "We are passing a nun riding
a bicycle."

  'He smiles gently. "That's not true, Muriel."

  'Mama flushes, avoiding the nun with a super-
human wrench of the great steering wheel. But she
says nothing.')

  'My father is blind,' she said suddenly. 'He was
blinded in the war, so all my life . . . he hasn't been
able to see.'

  'My grandmother was blind,' he said. 'She wore
glasses with dark blue lenses, like stained glass, but
the frames were gold. Rather pretty.'

  'My father,' she said desperately, 'doesn't have to
wear glasses. He doesn't look blind. He does everything for himself. He mows the lawn.'

  'My grandmother did embroidery. She distin-
guished the colours, she said, by touch.'

  'Where shall we have lunch?'

  'Right here.'

[43]

He turned the car into a parking lot in the centre of a small, apparently dead, town. When she crawled out, stretched, waited for him while he locked up, she heard no sound, saw no one.

'Like *High Noon*,' she said.

'You want a gun battle?'

They laughed, together, for the first time. He took her right arm; she could feel his hand on her arm, but not against her breast; she glanced at him, but he was still smiling. He led her over cobbles to the restaurant, which was called The Captain's Table. When they were inside, sitting on high pews under glowing ships' lanterns, abruptly plunged into midnight, he took his gloves off and laid them neatly on the table.

'Martini?'

'All right.'

'You feel well?'

'I feel fine.'

'Good.' He looked directly at her, his eyes not moving about her face but including all of it. 'You know something?'

'What?'

'Save it till later.' He was authoritative, rather brusque with the waitress. Again she felt a movement of distrust, suspicion. The martinis were powerful, so cold that they seemed to be steaming; she warmed the glass in her hands before drinking.

'My editor said, beware of martinis.'

'Your editor is a woman?'

She laughed, but hiding behind her glass. 'I suppose so.'

'You mean she is Lesbian?'

'No. I mean she's . . . well, nothing.'

'And you?'

'Me?'

'You have a husband? A lover of some sort?'

She finished the martini slowly, answered slowly. 'No. No, not at the moment.'

'That's not true, I'm sure of it.'

'Why should you say that?'

'Let's order. You want me to do it?'

That would be funny: a woman who couldn't order her own food. She breathed slowly into her martini glass, a child breathing on a frosted window. 'Please.'

He ordered baked clams, which she detested, and a local roast turkey which, he admitted sadly, was certainly not local. There were chilled glasses for the wine.

'They're very good at ice,' she said.

'Oh, surely. They refrigerate everything. Schizophrenics, spermatozoa, corpses.'

'You don't like them?'

'I've made my home here. Sure I like them.'

'Well, then.'

'I don't . . . feel very strongly. Where I can do my work and make most money, that's where I live.'

'Have you ever been back to Hungary?'

'No.'

'And your parents . . . ?'

'Dead. I have a sister, five years older than me. She lives in Sydney, Australia.'

'So you don't see her?'

'No. She married an Australian she met in Paris. But we write. You don't care for the clams?'

'Yes, but . . . I don't know, I'm not hungry. Do you go to Europe at all?'

'I was last there in 'sixty-two. I don't like it. We have your books, paintings, music, movies, theatre— why go to Europe?' Again he gave her the curiously inclusive, direct look, as though he had wide-focus eyes, without smiling. 'You know the story of the scorpion?'

'No.'

'It was in an old Orson Welles movie—I can't remember which one. The scorpion goes up to a frog on a river-bank and says, "Please take me across the river on your back." "You are crazy," says the frog, "you would sting me and I would drown." "It's you who's crazy," says the scorpion. "If I stung you when you were taking me across the river on your back, I should drown too." So the frog is persuaded, and the scorpion climbs on his back and off they go. Halfway across the river, the scorpion stings the frog. As they are both drowning, sinking down to the river-bed, the frog asks, "But *why*?" And the scorpion says, "Because it is my nature".'

'I think it's a . . . terrible story.'

'Yes. It is.'

'Are you the scorpion? Or the frog?'

He smiled. 'I told you a story, not a fable. They were simply a scorpion and a frog. You're not eating anything.'

[46]

'No, but I'm going to be plastered again. Like last night.'

'Last night you were tired. Don't you drink in England?'

'Yes, but . . . I suppose it's the martinis.'

'Of which your editor told you to beware.'

She laughed. 'That's right.'

They were sitting opposite each other, he eating, she leaning her elbows on the table. They had not moved any closer, or touched, but their whole physical relationship to each other had changed, was changing. What had been an indeterminate distance between their hands, knees, faces, was now measured exactly: they were accessible to each other. The martinis and the wine had dulled her panic, but she knew that if this went on, this almost imperceptible, inevitable meeting between them, if it wasn't stopped by the Sunday afternoon outside, the drive back, then somehow she must tell him; before it was too late she must probably watch an expression of horror and disgust, however momentary and well controlled, on his face; she must appear to believe his excuses, and not allow him to feel guilty. Not for his sake, but for her own, because the responsibility for making him feel guilty would last, she knew, far longer than his guilt.

He said, 'The scorpion was truthful.'

'In the end.'

'No. The whole thing was in his nature.'

'Even kidding the frog in the first place?'

'Of course.'

'Then it was really suicide.'

'If you like.'

'I feel more for the frog. Not understanding.'

'Do you?' He sounded sceptical. For a moment, as in the car, he looked at her eyes; against her will, she felt her eyes opening, deepening, taking him in; he seemed to search about in them, looking for some truth. She got up, banging her knees against the table leg, and went to the Ladies'. Standing there, with the Musak playing, she cupped her hand over the hard breast, viciously dug her fingers into it until the thought that she might puncture it with her fingernails frightened her. She wanted to cry; and at the same time, she didn't care. She was angry like a child, wanting to hurt and be hurt, to feel pain, to feel anything. Ramsey had a book called *The History of Torture Through the Ages* which showed, on the cover, a plump lady, with much the same benign expression as Sebastian, having her breast cut off with an enormous pair of scissors. I want to feel what she felt, I want to feel!

It was useless. Don't tell him; let it all go. But the resignation was only on the surface, it felt like cowardice. Underneath, the anger against herself raged brightly, a clear fire. She had never felt this anger before; she could never remember feeling it before. It was enlivening, making her very defined and sharp, as though she had become a weapon.

When she got back to the table he had paid the bill and was putting his gloves on. As they left the restaurant she looked back, trying to print it all in her mind, the lanterns and anchors and swags of rope,

knowing that she would never go there again, and
that it had been important to her.

*   *   *

On the way back, they were silent at first. He didn't
sing. He had tilted the mirror again, and looked into
it, at her, constantly. She told herself that she found
this rather a cheap trick; he would undoubtedly take
girls down to the country, in the Bentley or the
Ferrari, most weekends. They would be excited by
this attention—Rowan and Pat, the college girls of
the night before. At last she asked him, 'Do you . . .
have some girl?' realising that this sounded patron-
ising. He shrugged, then smiled at her. His smile was
very rare and more sad, in some way, than his normally
dogged and serious expression.

'There was an accident. Five months ago. My
fiancée was drowned.'

'Oh . . . I'm sorry.'

'I will tell you about it some day.'

'I'm leaving on Tuesday. We do a short tour of the
east coast.'

'How short?'

'Until Friday.'

'And then you will come back?'

'I don't know. We have . . . open returns. I mean,
after Friday night, we're on our own. I'll probably
go straight home.'

'Why?'

'Because I must work.'

'Yes. I see.'

[49]

'Will you tell me about it before Tuesday?'

'That is rather soon. I doubt it.'

'Yes,' she said. 'I understand that.'

The sun had gone, the colours drained away. She tried to think about the reception, the General, the journalists, Godfrey Wrench.

'I feel as though I'm going back to school.'

'You went to boarding school?'

'Yes, of course. We lived in the country, on my father's pension. So I went to a school for officers' children, which was very cheap.'

'You had no brothers or sisters?'

'No.'

'My sister was five years older than me. You know something? My father was quite well off, a lawyer as it happens, he hated to stay home. So every vacation we would go off on holiday. It was the most dreaded thing of my life. When I was eleven years old I had to share a hotel bedroom with my sister—Christmas, Easter and summer vacations, always with my sister. She was a big, blowzy girl—later she got thinner, but in those days she was like a Rubens, bulging and bursting out of everything. When she had her period I would put my head underneath the pillow and pray.'

'Pray?'

'I would say, "Oh God, let me not be here." Is that praying?'

'Yes.'

'My mother was sickly, she said nothing. We were allowed to order breakfast in our room, Monica and I, as this kept us out of the way of my father, who would eat an English breakfast in the dining-room, napkin in his collar, reading the continental *Daily Telegraph*. The waiter would wheel in our breakfast through the piles of nylon panties . . .'

'Oh, no.'

'The drifts of grey broderie anglaise. Monica loved broderie anglaise. I would shift five brassières off the chair and sit down in my flannel pyjamas and try to eat. There was hair in the coffee, face powder in the jam. Of course I loved my sister. But oh my God, she smelled!'

She was laughing, although the story was tragic. 'How long did this go on?'

'I think it would have gone on for ever. We would have been married by now. But I escaped when I was sixteen, and went to Paris. There I learned that I knew a great deal about women. A great deal—and nothing at all.'

'How did you escape?'

'That's another story.'

'All right. And Monica?'

'Married an Australian, as I told you. She sent me a picture. She is now reaching forty and has two daughters.'

'Could we stop somewhere? We have time. I'd like a coffee.'

'Of course.'

'What did you feel—when you were trapped in all those brassières and broderie anglaise?'

'I don't know. I remember thinking there was nowhere else to go.'

'But downstairs—to your father?'

'He was reading the continental *Daily Telegraph*.'

'Your mother?'

'Well. She wasn't so interesting.'

He drew up in front of a small store, which called itself a Post Office. Inside it was packed from floor to ceiling with groceries and toys and tablecloths, plastic buckets and pocket knives, mirrors and potato chips, ten-gallon hats and stockings and hams in pink cellophane. The proprietor, a dark, burly man, didn't speak; possibly, they thought, he was dumb. They sat at the post-office counter on small, worn stools. The proprietor's daughter, in black stockings, made Instant Coffee. Her small brother, about five years old, walked carefully to and fro with great piles of clean plates, which he stored away under the counter. Nobody spoke. Muriel and Robert leant on the counter with their arms touching, looking into their coffee as they stirred it. The little store was very warm, smelt of wood shavings and soap powder, it seemed dedicated to silence. The little boy went away and didn't come back. They looked at each other gravely.

'Listen . . .'

He put his hand over hers, but almost immediately took it away again.

'No,' he said. 'I don't want to listen.'

'I want to tell you something.'

'You don't have to tell me anything.'

'I don't have to. But I want to.'

'Then tell me.'

She laughed shortly, pushing the skin up over her cheek-bones, pressing her fingers into her cheek-bones. 'Now I can t.'

'Look,' he said quietly, 'there's nothing you need to tell me. You are who you are, here, now, to me. That's all that matters.'

'To you. Not to me.'

'Then I'm sorry.'

'I've never told anyone before.'

'Then please, please don't.'

'Because it's never been necessary. Perhaps it's not necessary now. That's what's so silly.'

He spread out his hands, exasperated. 'You are really a man.'

'No. I had cancer. I . . . had an operation.' She touched her breast. 'There it is.'

His eyes were perfectly steady. He was even very faintly smiling. 'How long ago?'

'In May.'

'In May. That was quite a month for us. Both breasts, or just one?'

'Oh . . . just one.'

'And the doctors were quite satisfied with you? It's all over?'

'They say they're quite sure. Yes.'

'Does it upset you?'

'Upset me? Of course it does. Of course it does.'

'Then if you don't mind me saying so, which you certainly will, you are making a foolish fuss.' Suddenly he leant towards her and gave her a quick, childish kiss on the lips. 'You have been saved from a very terrible illness, and you are upset. Come on . . .'

'Hell, oh hell, I want to cry.'

'No, you don't. You want a brandy in that unpleasant coffee, and then to go back to your delightful

[53]

colleagues and write some more in your notebook and go to your party, and tonight, if you will allow me, I will come and fetch you for a drink and you can see the pigsty where I live.'

He seemed to be far away, wavering, distorted, as though the tears in her eyes were fathoms deep. She said, 'I'm sorry.'

'Now you are irritating me.'

'Then I'll keep quiet.'

'Yes. Let's be quiet.'

They sat at the post-office counter with their arms touching, looking down into their coffee, peaceful.

4

BILL ANDERSON said, 'We missed you today, Muriel.'

'Did you . . . Bill?'

'How was your day, then?'

'Oh, fine. Lovely.'

Godfrey Wrench came up to them, holding a glass of orange juice. 'We missed you today, Muriel.'

'Did you, Godfrey?'

'How was your day, then?'

'Fine. We went out into the country. How was your day?'

'Apart from the leaves, abominable.'

'Oh, I wouldn't say that,' Bill Anderson said. 'I wouldn't say that.'

'You look, if I might say so, transported,' Godfrey said gently.

'Thank you, Godfrey.'

A man she didn't know, but had seen on the plane, came up to them. He was middle-aged and eager, his shirt-cuffs frayed. 'Good evening, Muriel. We missed you today.'

'I'm sorry. I feel rather guilty.'

'My name's Frogmore, Wallace. I understand you work for the General?'

'Well . . . yes.'

'Amazing woman, that. You know her, Wrench? Great class. You're a lucky girl, Muriel. And how are you liking it in the New World?'

'Very much,' she said. 'Who are we meant to be meeting?'

'Just a lot of art types,' Frogmore said. 'Let's hope that tomorrow we can get down to it and find out how this city really works. You've got your interviews lined up, Muriel?'

'Yes,' she lied. 'All lined up.'

'Well, then,' Frogmore said, 'on with the motley.' He went purposefully off through the crowd.

'Now I'm back again,' she said.

'I don't know if you've seen this house. It's rather beautiful—seventeenth century, remarkably well restored. Come and have a look.'

As she followed Wrench up the stairs, she looked at her watch, counted the remaining hours—three. She wanted to sit down by herself and think, try to realise, try to understand what she had done. They had parted casually; he had said he would pick her up at eleven outside the hotel. Could she telephone him, say she had changed her mind? Lock herself in her room, write him a letter? She could do none of those things; she had told him, and he had accepted it, the deal was completed, there was no longer any way out. She wondered what would happen if she put the situation to Wrench—an irrational, childish hope that he might deal with it for her, go and explain to Robert, smooth it all over. They reached a large, low room with a shining pine floor, a great fire, polished cedarwood and walnut glowing.

'All the window fittings—bolts and so on—were taken from an old nunnery. The glazing is eighteenth century.'

'How do you know so much about it?'

'I've been here for half an hour. What else is there to do?'

'Have you got your interviews lined up for tomorrow?'

'Oh . . . rubbish.'

He came and sat down beside her. She felt the fire scorching her shins. He looked at her sideways. 'Well?'

'Well?'

'I've read some of your pieces. They're very intelligent, considering.'

'Considering what?'

'Well, that rag you work for. Why don't you get a decent job?'

'Like what?'

'We'd take you on.'

'On the Woman's Page?'

'Probably. But you could write other stuff.'

'I don't know. I'm kind of . . . obligated.'

'To that hideous woman? Don't be childish. You're obligated to yourself, that's all. Ever thought of writing a novel?'

Another lie: 'No. Of course not.'

'So what were you writing in the plane for two hours? Cookery hints?'

She sat up straight, looking round, fussing. 'I'm sure we shouldn't be sitting up here like this. Shouldn't we be mixing?'

'If you like.'

'All right. I don't want to. But I don't want to talk about writing, either. What's this theology?'

'Largely writing.'

'I meant mine, not yours.'

'Well . . . I'm very interested in what you might call religious behaviour.'

'Are you religious?'

'Yes.'

'Catholic?'

'Yes. Well . . . for the last four years. Before that . . . drifting.'

'I see.' She spread out her hands, although they weren't cold, and watched the firelight shine through the thin skin between her fingers. 'I never know what to say.'

'That's all right. Why should you say anything?'

'I feel as though you'd suddenly said . . . you were quite different from me. Not just foreign . . . but altogether different.'

'That's probably true.'

'You believe it all? About divorce, contraception, abortion, the whole lot?'

'There are more important things. But yes, I believe the Church's teaching about all that.'

'I don't understand. I mean . . . you deliberately make yourself believe things which you must know are nonsense, you must know they're not true. I'm sorry. That sounds very arrogant.'

[58]

'But,' he said, 'I don't know they're nonsense, and I don't think they're not true. On the contrary.'

'Well. You're married . . .'

'Since our youngest child was born, I've been celibate, if that's what you mean.'

'For . . . ?'

'Three years.'

'But your wife . . .?'

'She agrees with me. She understands.'

'For three years? Always? All the time?'

'One falls from grace occasionally.' He said it with a total lack of pomposity, as though admitting to a harmless, even frivolous, failing.

'And then what?'

'What does the song say? "Pick yourself up, dust yourself off, start all over again." Someday, with any luck, it will be possible.'

'But why?'

'Partly because we don't want any more children. Partly . . . discipline.'

'I lived with someone, a man, for three years. He's married and his wife won't divorce him. I suppose you'd say that was sinful?'

He made a gentle, deprecating gesture, as much as to say not necessarily.

'It must have been, the way you look at things. But would it have been less sinful if I'd had three children during that time? Was it worse because . . . I had a bit of nylon put inside me, so that whatever happened would just happen to us?'

'And what did happen?'

'We broke up. I told you.'

He said nothing.

'You think if we'd had children we'd have stayed together. But then what about his wife? What could we have done, that you would think right—I mean, apart from refusing to live together?'

'My dear girl, I'm not judging you.'

'Yes, you are. You must be. If you know what's right, and don't judge, what good is it?'

'You mean, you want me to judge you?'

She laughed uncomfortably. She wanted him, of course, to tell her not to go to Robert. However nonsensical the reason, she would have accepted it.

'Of course not. I'm sorry.'

'Anyway, with your little piece of nylon, these things hardly concern you, do they? You can just have a good time, and the hell with it.'

'You're jealous.'

'Probably.'

She said, 'I like you anyway.'

'Good. I like you too.'

While they had been talking, a crowd of people had come upstairs, the room was full. Godfrey said, 'Isn't that your Bentley friend?'

'No. Where?' Then she saw him, in his brown suit; he looked directly at her, but hardly smiled. 'Yes.' She felt abruptly angry, as though Robert were a warder, a body-guard, owning her. 'What the hell is he doing here?'

'Why shouldn't he be here?'

'He wasn't invited.'

'Oh, come on. What's the matter with you?'

'I don't know. Let's go and meet someone. That's what we're here for.'

'What happened to you today? What's biting you?'

'Nothing.' Like a pestered child, are you tired, are you happy, have you had enough, would you like some more, which do you want, what would you like to do? She got up, leaving Godfrey to follow if he felt like it. As she edged across the room, Robert came up to her.

'Hullo.'

'Hullo.'

'I thought you might want to be rescued. Go to a movie or something.'

'We have to go to dinner.'

'Have to?'

'Yes.'

He stepped aside, inclining his head slightly. 'Then I'll see you later.'

'I don't know. Yes, maybe . . . I don't know . . .'

'I'll wait outside the hotel, anyway. About eleven.'

Godfrey was behind her. He said, 'I'm told Alex MacNeish is just leaving, if you want to meet him.'

'Yes. Yes, of course I do.' Going down the stairs, she asked, 'Who is Alex MacNeish?'

5

'THERE is an obsessive tenderness and passion, an eating out of one's heart, a sense of longing, an affliction, which remains buried and unchanged from childhood, this is what is called falling in love. The longing is for reciprocation, the affliction is in knowing that reciprocation is forbidden. No mother can love her son, no father his daughter, as they need to be loved. If they could, the world would come to an end. But the end of the world becomes a possibility in this state of innocence, love is fatal, a sickness, a falling, it breaks the heart; at the same time, to feel such hidden emotions, to be swept and shaken by them, releases a liveliness like fire. At the moment this passion is requited, and so-called normal sexual expression permitted, it fades, either disappearing entirely, or being replaced by strong feelings of sexual attraction and affection, love itself. While it lasts, it is responsible for the most poignant extremes of feeling, raising the possessed person to the skies or plunging him into the depths; it is an occupation, an inspiration, and can become, in certain unstable personalities, a madness. . . .'

That's all very well, but what brings it on, this affliction? Why for one person and not another? Why at first sight, the sense of being done for? Is it that at that particular moment sadness, or anger, or dullness, have reached a point where they have to be . . . what, neutralised, corrected? Chemical? Why that particular head, voice, expression, why so catastrophically sudden? No question of choice. He turns, holds your right hand for a moment, smiles, you have known him all your life; it even seems possible that you have known him for ever.

'Miss Rowbridge . . . Alex MacNeish.'

'Hullo.'

'Hullo.'

'I was just leaving.'

'I know. They told me.'

'Oh? Why? I mean, why did they tell you?'

'Not just me . . .'

'What did they say?'

'They said I should meet you.'

'That's very nice of them. You come from England.'

'Yes.'

'So do I.'

'Really? I thought . . .'

'Oh no, I've been over here for about ten years, but I often go back. I was there this summer. You live in London?'

'Yes.'

'Whereabouts?'

'In . . . well, in Bayswater really.'

'We had a house in Hyde Park Square. That's Bayswater, isn't it?'

[63]

'Yes, I suppose it is. It just sounds . . . grander.'

'It was good for the kids, the girl could just take them over to the Park, they liked that.'

'How old are they?'

'Four and six, boys. Are you married?'

'No.'

'A writer?'

'Well . . . yes.'

'What d'you mean, "Well . . . yes"? Either you are or you aren't.'

'Yes. I am.'

'What do you write?'

'I'm a journalist. I'm with this . . . party.'

'But you write something else? Novels? Stories? You're going to?'

'Yes. Yes, I do.'

'What d'you write about? No, that's a silly question. Are you going to have dinner?'

'I think we're all meant to be going. Why don't you come too?'

'No. No, I'm no good at that sort of thing. Joss has something ready at home. I thought you might have liked to come along.'

'Perhaps I could . . .'

'No, you'd better stick with your party. How long are you staying?'

'Till Tuesday.'

'Not long.'

'No. I might come back again. Next weekend.'

'Well, if you do . . . let's meet.'

'Perhaps we could have lunch. Before then. On Tuesday.'

'All right. I should be through post-synching by Tuesday, if I'm not I'll ring you. Come to the office around one. O.K.?'

He tore the flap off an envelope and scribbled the address. She put it into her handbag, said, 'All right. Tuesday, then.' She looked at him for a moment with a kind of alarm, feeling that she could in reality say, Don't leave me, stay with me, be with me. Then she smiled, turned to look for Godfrey, the first of the many deceits that seem necessary to someone who has fallen in love.

At dinner she was put between Wallace Frogmore and the news editor of a local paper. The two men had a great deal to say to each other, so that she spent the meal pressed back in her chair, or crouched forward over her enormous steak, thankfully silent. Godfrey was pinioned by somebody's wife, a blonde grand-daughter of some forgotten revolution whose voice cut down the centre of the table like an electric saw. She thought her watch had stopped then found that what she had thought was half an hour had in fact been five minutes.

He has blue eyes, set rather close to his nose; a small mouth; greying hair. Stocky, with elegant hands. He wore a brown wool shirt, no tie, suède jacket, good clothes, well looked after: alligator, buckskin, calf, chamois, crocodile, doeskin, goatskin, kid, lizard, morocco, pigskin, sheepskin, suède, clothed all in leather, but soft, even to the shoes. I wouldn't think, from his accent, that he was English; but when he told me, realised that of course he was English, a quiet voice. Joss: she is a good wife, cooks his food in the evenings, but is too busy to take the children to the Park. She knows him very well, sometimes dislikes him, they quarrel, I take no sides, she is nothing to do with me. Post-synching is something to do with synchronising sound, so that the characters in the film say what they appear to be saying. He has a great many awards; in his home there will be a cupboard or shelves full of small reclining and upright women, marble and onyx; posters, I expect, and certificates of honour, probably in the bathroom. His handwriting is more childish than mine. We could have sat here all night. At some time during the night we would have parted, to meet tomorrow.

'Heard from our Lady Clarissa?' Wallace Frogmore asked. 'Been in touch, have you?'

'No. No, I haven't.'

'I call the office every day. Bloody drag, nothing to tell them, all food and drink so far. I had jaundice last year.'

'Did you?'

'Very bad go of it. You're not eating much, I see.'

'No.'

'Had a slap-up lunch, I suppose, while we were all driving round looking at those bloody leaves?'

The man is a complete stranger: 'I thought you might like to come along . . . Well, if you do, let's meet. If I'm not through, I'll ring you.' Perhaps this happens, something they didn't tell me, perhaps one goes a little mad. She smiled at Frogmore as they talked, thinking it's just a question of post-synchronisation. My mouth is saying yes, I had a very nice lunch thank you, and I am saying that in an hour or so I'm going to be taken off, or have arranged to have myself taken off in a Ferrari or a Bentley to the flat of a company lawyer whom I don't know when I have just fallen, fallen in with a man with whom I want to spend hours, days, weeks; but not nights.

'There's no night-life,' Wallace Frogmore said.

'We'll have to prove you wrong there,' the news editor said.

'Oh well, in that case . . . Want to come along, Muriel?'

'No. No, thank you.'

The party was breaking up. Godfrey came up to her, looking haggard.

'Going back to the hotel?'

'Yes.'

'Let's walk. It's only a couple of blocks.'

They said goodbye. The news editor was telling Wallace Frogmore that they would go to the Frug-a-Gogo and find a coupla chicks. Bill Anderson looked lonely and disapproving. The night was cold, clear, their footsteps echoed. If she had thought that Godfrey would explain, help her, she was wrong. They walked in silence for most of the way, then he said, 'He seemed a nice fellow, MacNeish. Very talented.'

'Yes.'

'He was in Venice a couple of years ago, with his wife and kids. Very attractive woman, I think she's an actress.'

'Oh, really?'

'I enjoyed our talk, by the way.'

'Yes. So did I.'

In the foyer of the hotel he said good night. She took her key and went up to her room, to get ready.

6

THE flat was unexpected, crammed with furnish-
ing. There were a great many books, but other-
wise not a painting, picture, object on view that
told her anything about the man. They sat in over-
upholstered chairs in the living-room, among what
seemed a forest of silk lampshades, and drank Scotch
on ice from tall glasses. The record-player was
playing Aznavour, Montand, Beçaud, a continuous
subdued howl of melancholy French erotica. The
reason for her being there seemed so obvious that
she wanted to get on with it. Aznavour and Scotch
won't soften me up; I'm as soft now as I'll ever
be with you, tough as a plastic skin, hard as a
bag of water, calling for someone who can't hear
me.

She asked, 'Do you know Alex MacNeish?'

'No. No, I don't. Not personally. He was there
tonight.'

'Yes. I talked to him.'

'You did? I like his work very much. You found
him interesting?'

'Yes. Yes, very interesting.'

'His wife is an excellent actress—Josephine Carrier,

you have seen her in his films, they work together a great deal.'

'Oh. Oh, I . . . don't remember.'

As though she were new to feeling, each wave of happiness, excitement, anger and now desolation was an onslaught for which she was unprepared. She had, in the last few seconds, renounced a man who worked with his wife, for to work with a wife was more formidable than loving her, living with her, sleeping with her. Now, in this childlike state, unable to express her confusion, she felt a sudden longing for Ramsey, for anyone who had known her to be rational, ordinary and undeformed.

She said, 'Robert, listen, I . . .'

He came over and held her shoulders. His hands were warm, two clamps holding her together.

'Quiet . . . Will you never be quiet?'

'But I . . .'

He kissed her. *He knows about me and he is real. This has never happened before, I can't run away.* But she could not pull him towards her or press herself against him, the barrier was too great. It was she who said, 'Let's go, then.'

He got up immediately and went into the next room, not waiting for her. He came back with a bath-robe, which he dropped on an armchair. Presumably she was meant to undress in the living-room —delicacy? She took the robe into the bedroom, but found him turning down the bed. Looking for the bathroom, she found herself in the kitchen—orange peel and egg shells, dirty glasses collected over the weekend. She heard him flush the lavatory, so went quickly into the bedroom. He was cleaning his teeth in the bathroom. She took a great mouthful of Scotch and held it in her mouth, a little dribbled out and she wiped her mouth on the back of her hand, swallowing. Undress, for God's sake! She pulled off her clothes as though they were on fire, leaving them in a heap on the floor, struggling into the bath-robe as she heard him come out of the bathroom and switch off the light. He went into the living-room and there was silence for a couple of minutes: he had put on another record, how many records, what would happen when they came to an end? She wished, for the first time since going into hospital, that she could have a cigarette. He came in, wearing a robe like her own, his legs and chest brown and hairy; he offered her a cigarette and she took it, lit it, coughed, spluttered, stubbed it out with her eyes streaming and shaking her head from side to side to gain breath.

'Not used to it,' she said.

He smiled. 'I'm sorry.' He sat down on the bed, legs crossed, leaning against the wall, perfectly patient.

'They told me to give it up in case . . .'

'Yes. I understand.'

'But I wanted one.'

He took something out of his pocket. 'Catch.'

She caught it—a smooth, egg-shaped crystal. 'What's it for?'

'Holding.'

'Oh.'

She was standing in the middle of the room. He leant forward and gently held out his hand, as though encouraging a child to walk. She took his hand, her

[71]

other holding the crystal, and came to stand in front
of him.

'All right?'

She nodded.

'Take off the robe, please.'

Her fist closed round the crystal, she didn't move.

'Take off the robe.'

She realised afterwards that she had expected him to
do this for her, as though she were indeed a child.
She took her hand away from his, undid the belt,
the robe hung loose.

'Off,' he said, patiently.

She shrugged it off and stood in front of him,
clenching the crystal in her right hand.

'Thank you,' he said.

Without holding her, he put his face against her
stomach, almost as though he were looking into her.
Then his dry, closed lips moved along the crease of
her stomach, from hip bone to hip bone. She looked
down at his head below the smooth, pale concavity
of her chest; her free hand moved to his head, touched
it gently, found his face, raised his face, made him look
at her. He was troubled, anxious. She smiled broadly,
taking his hand and holding it against her breast; his
other hand moved slowly upwards, exploring with
palm and fingers the wonder of her bone and unbroken
skin.

'You're beautiful.'

'Odd.'

'No, not odd. Beautiful.'

She felt again what she had felt at lunchtime—an
anger so sharp, so delicate and lively, that it was

almost love. 'Smile, then. Don't . . . take me seriously.'

He pulled her abruptly on to the bed. Their love-making had some tenderness, but its truth, for both of them, lay in this anger of hers, this sense of triumph.

*   *   *

'So you are going away?'

'Yes.'

'Where to?'

'I don't know. Dreary places. Somewhere called Pembroke. Then Civic Centres and Cultural Complexes—I don't know.'

'Maybe I'll come and see you.'

'In the Ferrari or the Bentley?'

'Either or both.'

'I wish you would.'

'Then I will. I'll fetch you back here again, at the end of the week.'

'But I must go home.'

'Why?'

'All right. We're going to the Canyons and the Falls, probably the Gobi Desert. How will you find me?'

'I'll find you. We'll go and take the boat in, over the weekend.'

'Oh, your boat . . . Tell me now. You promised you'd tell me.'

'Not now. Later.'

'I'm sorry. I didn't think. Half the time I don't think. I'm sorry.'

'It's all right. I don't mind talking about it. Just now . . .'

'Where's the crystal?'

'Gone.'

'We must find it.'

'Martha will find it in the morning.'

'Your char?'

'My cleaning woman. She has a Sunbeam Alpine.'

'What is it about you and cars? What would I have, for instance?'

'A Facel Vega. With only one wing. Exceptionally swift and beautiful.'

'In fact I had a Mini. And that wasn't mine.'

'Your husband's?'

'I never had a husband.'

'Your lover's, then.'

'Yes. His wife doesn't drive. There is an army of mini-cab drivers all over London who get paid in kind for taking her to Blackheath.'

'I'm sorry. I don't understand.'

'It doesn't matter. You know—with my disability, I ought to be nicer.'

'Why?'

'Blindness made my father nicer, I'm sure of it. He can see everybody's point of view. Trouble is, he can't see.'

'Give me a drink. No, no, like this . . .'

'My grandmother used to tell me . . . that her mother gave her lollipops like this . . . More?'

'No. I'm drowning . . .'

*   *   *

LADY CLARISSA BIRD INGHAMS PRESS LONDON EC4
ALL SWINGING AVOIDING V WOOLF SEE YOU MONDAY
IF UNDELAYED BY REDSKINS
MURIEL

'Wolf?' the clerk spelled out, at five o'clock.
'Redskins?'
'That's right. It's a joke.'
'Ah. I get it. Good night, then, miss.'
'It's a fine day outside,' she said. 'And morning.'

7

The telephone, screaming in her ear like a siren: she groped for it, knocked it over, found the receiver chattering on the floor: 'Hello? Hello?'

'Yes,' she said, 'what is it?'

'Miss Rowbridge? This is Anna Palmer, Press Representative of the Women's Guild. I was meeting you at nine-thirty in the lobby, if you remember.'

'Were you? I mean, are you? What's the time?'

'It is now quarter to ten. I imagined you had been delayed.'

'That's right. I was . . .'

'We have an appointment at the new infant school out in Roseberry at ten-thirty. You think you can make it?'

'I'll be down in five minutes—can you wait?'

'I'll expect you, then.'

Oh no, oh no, the new infant school—curiously formed, perhaps, colourful, flying infants, like nothing she had seen before? She dragged back the curtains, stumbled to the bathroom, put her whole head under the cold shower. The telephone rang again; she found her way to it with a towel over her face, hair streaming.

'Yes?'

'Good morning.'

'Oh, it's you. Look, the most awful thing—I'm dead asleep and I have to be at the new infant school at Roseberry.'

'For God's sake, why?'

'I don't know why. But there's a woman from some Guild waiting down in the lobby, she talks entirely in the past tense.'

'Then leave her in the past tense. Go back to sleep and we'll have lunch very late.'

'I can't, Robert.'

'All right. Will you call me?'

'I don't know when.'

'It doesn't matter. I'll be there. You know something?'

'What?'

'I'll tell you later.'

When she was dressed she felt more like a half-drowned delinquent than a representative of the Englishwoman's press—pale face, smudged eyes, dripping hair, even a small hole in the knee of her stocking, such betrayal, such disloyalty. She grabbed yesterday's handbag, which didn't match, because the notebook was already in it, and ran towards the lift. She was on the eleventh floor, so the journey was fairly long and peaceful. She leant against the lift wall and slowly remembered the night; then realised that this was the first time that she had woken, and dressed, without any sense of mourning.

Anna Palmer was surprised, no doubt of that. She wore a silk two-piece, slip-over coat with kimono sleeves and a helmet of nylon rose-petals.

'We have quite a heavy schedule, Muriel—I can call you, Muriel, can't I? We want you to see everything that women are doing for women in this city of ours. We want you to meet all kinds, from the President of our Guild to those who protest against Vietnam, for there are some rebels among us, believe me.' They climbed into a car with a tired-looking male driver. 'We believe that you women in Great Britain tend to think of us as just the slightest bit—old-fashioned? Maybe you think we're still driving the ole covered waggon and fighting the Injuns'—she laughed prettily—'but we want you to write about us as we really are, Muriel, and while we don't want to forget those days, which made us what we are, we do want to impress on you people in Europe that the average woman on this side of the ocean is as smart, maybe smarter, than any of your girls in Bond Street or the House of Commons. . . .'

Muriel listened with avid attention; she listened like someone trying to solve a trick question or spot the obvious mistake; she listened as though it were a memory test.

'Now I believe you women in Britain don't form yourselves into any undenominational union, as we do. Catholics, Protestants, Jews, coloured or white, are all welcome in the Guild—so long, of course, as they're happy, though we do have more specialised groups for those who don't feel altogether at ease, for if there's one thing we do believe in it's freedom of thought and speech and action for women everywhere. I'm proud to tell you, Muriel, that only a couple of months ago two thousand members of the

Guild from every walk of life signed a public letter to President Johnson supporting the Civil Rights Bill. Now I don't know what equivalent you have for this in Great Britain, but I rather doubt if your Prime Minister gets quite such a package as that in his morning mail!'

'No,' Muriel said.

'Now we're starting with the Roseberry Infants' School because we have to face the fact, Muriel, that unless our young women can turn over their kids with complete confidence, unless their own minds are entirely at rest, you can have all the emancipation and franchise in the world—the kitchen sink will win the day. That's one of your telling phrases, now, isn't it?'

'I'm sorry. What?'

'Kitchen sink. It comes in one of those marvellous plays by George Bernard Shaw about women's rights—*Candida* or *Major Barbara*, I feel certain.'

'Yes, of course. I'm not very bright this morning, I'm sorry.'

'The air, I guess. You're used to all that fog in London. Though, mind you, it's humid today.'

'Humid?'

'We call it anti-complexion weather—very bad if you happen to have enlarged pores. Anyway, as I was saying, the infant school is the basis of our whole drive, so we thought it natural to start there. Roseberry was built at the cost of some five million dollars, one-third of this put up by the Municipality, the rest by private contribution, and it was completed in June of this year. At the moment it takes around eight hundred and seventy infants, liberating seven hundred

[79]

and fifty mothers into the wage-earning category . . .'

'Is it compulsory?' Muriel asked weakly.

'Well, sure, education is compulsory after the age of five. There are a few private nurseries, of course, that cater for children before that age—I believe this is very common practice in your country, but we rather tend to frown on it here. We feel that motherhood is the greatest experience that can happen to any woman and that unless she gets her child standing firmly on its feet—and I mean this literally, Muriel—before pushing it off to school, why then she is depriving herself of the happiest years of her life and we all know what *that* means.'

Perhaps I'm not hearing correctly; perhaps I'm still drunk; perhaps—oh, what a hope, what a marvel —Anna Palmer is drunk. She turned and looked at Anna Palmer carefully. Anna Palmer rapped the driver on the shoulder.

'Here, driver, here!' She got out of the car delicately, with an extended navy court shoe and slim veined leg, a swish of terylene. 'Wait for us, please.'

Muriel looked at the driver, but he didn't look at her. He unfolded a comic from his pocket and slapped it open against the wheel.

In the infants' school, which was a marvellously imaginative piece of architecture, whoever had paid for it, Muriel revived a little. The infants were grave or raucous, according to their mood, and moved with the determination of rock climbers over the great spaces that had been designed for their play. The teachers appeared to leave them alone, except to stand like guides at various danger points; then they were clear with their advice, and seemed undisturbed when it wasn't taken. An ideal world: you pummel your clay, carve your granite, hurl your paint at the Sistine ceiling, write your laborious words, bang on the kettledrum—a haven from nine till six, a world of poetry invaded by Anna Palmer. She wandered away from Anna Palmer, who was briskly ruffling any tidy head that came within her reach, and sat almost sleeping by the sand-pit. Images of the past twenty-four hours drifted through her as though she were dreaming—walking down the stairs with Godfrey, the stranger's back and shoulders, waiting indifferently for him to turn round, the shock of pleasure; Robert's body, urging her to come alive, to use her fear and anger instead of holding it inside; the sense of relief, now, as though a spell had been broken; speculation, fantasy about tomorrow, let's go to Guadeloupe, Acapulco, yes, I have my passport . . .

'We had an appointment with Yves Pretin at noon,' Anna Palmer said accusingly. 'For cocktails.'

'Did we?'

'If you have seen everything you care to see here, we should go.'

'Who's Eve Pretin?'

'Our most famous couturier. That is, dress designer. His salon is downtown, just by your hotel. Surely you have heard of Pretin?'

'Oh yes, of course. A man?'

'In a woman's world,' Anna Palmer said. She added naughtily, 'Well, you might say half and half.'

'Yes,' Muriel said patiently, getting up from the sand-pit. 'I understand.'

[81]

The driver folded his comic, they settled themselves in the car, Muriel yawned enormously, needing both hands to cover it.

'I was afraid you were tired,' Anna Palmer said, without much sympathy. 'I suppose the entertainment for you visiting press people is pretty lavish.'

Muriel opened her eyes a little wider and pitched her voice one tone higher; it felt as though she was making a supreme effort. 'This Yves Pretin—does he design for wholesalers—off-the-peg clothes that girls can buy in the shops?'

'Oh my goodness, no. He's *very* exclusive. Why, one gown from Yves can cost you as much as fifteen hundred dollars.'

'Then he doesn't really have much appeal for,' she took a great breath, 'the woman in the street?'

'Well, you could say that, looked at in one way. But when your Queen appears in a beautiful Hartnell gown—surely that's a delight for every woman?'

'Not really,' Muriel said.

'I'm sorry?'

'What do we do after Yves Pretin?'

'Well, the President is expecting you for a small, informal lunch party, and after that, around two-thirty, we shall be visiting the new housing complex on Luxborough. This complex houses over a thousand families—you'll find it just fascinating. Then around five we've arranged a little get-together with some of the girls from our top women's journals, they'll be asking you a few questions, I guess, and of course they're dying to tell you how we do things here and compare notes. Many of them have met Lady Clarissa—we all think she's such a very, very lovely person, don't you agree?—but they are, of course, just fascinated to meet a real working press woman like themselves, with the same problems and the same, well, background. They're all college girls, of course—I expect you're a college girl yourself, Muriel?'

She nodded, dumb. Words started going through her brain like a tune: Lord support us all the day long of this troublous life till the shadows lengthen and the evening comes the fever of life over and our work done . . . Lord support us all the day long of this troublous life . . .

'Are you sure you're feeling quite well, Muriel? Muriel, are you feeling okay?'

Again she nodded. Then Lord in thy mercy grant us safe lodging, holy rest and peace at the last through Jesus Christ's sake Amen . . . Lord support us all the day long of this troublous life then Lord in thy mercy grant us safe lodging, holy rest and peace at the last . . .

'Would you like to stop by at the hotel and fix your face . . . or anything?'

'No, thank you, Anna. I'm fine, Anna.'

'Good. That's good. A martini will fix you up in no time.'

Till the shadows lengthen and the evening comes the evening comes the evening comes the fever over . . .

A commissionaire welcomed Anna Palmer; Muriel stumbled through the door behind her. Going up the wide, blue-carpeted stairs, clinging to the gilded banister, she took a quick look at herself in the mirrored wall and was happy to recognise herself: a friend. A squat man in a mauve suit and a square beard welcomed Anna with open arms that strained his buttons.

'Anna! Doll!' He made straining noises as he kissed her, trying to excrete love. 'And this is . . . ?' He took it all in, and veiled his eyes.

'This is Muriel, from England. She's on a Press visit over here.'

'Muriel from England. That's a long, long way to come.'

'And I haven't weathered the journey very well, have I?' Support us all the day long.

'Pardon me, dear? My, you English, you have the quaintest language. Don't you think the English have the quaintest language, Anna?'

'I think I'll just . . .'

'Down the stairs and second door on the right,' Anna whispered. 'You'll find everything you need there. I'll wait for you, dear.'

She ran down the stairs without knees, her legs fluid from thigh to ankle. Holy rest and peace at the last I'll find there. She slipped through the heavy front door, bowed to the commissionaire and started running. Suddenly she was face to faceless with Reclining Woman, green as mildew, haughty as iron. Supporting herself against the plinth, she orientated herself, then walked very slowly and deliberately towards the hotel. General, forgive me, for I know exactly what I do. It comes from going to a school for

the daughters of disabled officers. I am a hopeless
failure all the day long.

'Don't put through any calls to my room, please.'

'A Mr. Wrench was asking for you, ma'am. He
said to tell you that he'd be in the cemetery.'

'The *cemetery*?'

'Well, it sounds kinda gruesome, I suppose, but it's
one of the city's beauty spots, ma'am.'

'How long ago? When did he go?'

'Around eleven, I guess. Said he'd wait for you until
one, said he'd be by the mausoleum. That's a very
fine building, you should see it . . .'

'Before I die, you mean?'

He was still laughing as she got into the lift, see it
before I die, man that's rich, see it before I die!

*   *   *

The taxi drove hearse-like along the broad avenues
of the cemetery, through the rioting trees; it climbed
in bottom gear between the vaults and sarcophagi
towards the marzipan Sacré Cœur at the top of the
hill. Below, the city lay in a blue haze, splashed with
flashes of metal and the burning leaves. With a clean
face and clean hair, back in her sweater and trousers,
hands smooth with lotion, unconstricted, she lay back
in the taxi and nodded amiably at the tombs, as
though the dead were congratulating her.

He was standing outside the mausoleum, reading
a pamphlet and eating a hot dog.

'I thought you'd probably be tied up with the
women's mags and so on.'

'I was. I ran away. Well. Not exactly ran away. I left.'

'Walked out on them?'

'I suppose so.'

'You don't mind?'

'Not much.'

'What about your job?'

'You've offered me one, remember?'

'Mm.' He sounded doubtful. 'You want a hot dog?'

'Yes. Do they give them out with the wafers?'

'You can,' he said, 'be a great deal funnier than that.'

He didn't pay for the hot dog. That was fair. They sat on the steps and ate, silently.

'Why did you come here?' she asked finally.

'Part of my research—cemeteries.'

'Why?'

He shrugged. 'I don't know. How people behave towards the dead.'

'And how do they behave?'

'Well . . . on the whole, they try to make it entertaining.'

'Death entertaining?'

'Why not?'

'The way people die isn't particularly entertaining.'

'I didn't say it was.'

'Oh . . . all right.' She smiled at him briefly and lay back on the steps, resting on her elbows, stretching her legs as far as they would go. 'It's nice here.'

'Yes. I thought you'd like it.'

'Aren't you doing any work?'

'I already saw the Mayor, the Chief of Police and three Senators. Won't that do for today?'

'I should think so. How were they?'

'The Mayor was interesting, the others predictable. You want to walk a bit?'

'What about the mausoleum?'

'I wouldn't advise it—1890 hysteria, not even funny. But if you want to . . .'

'No, let's walk.'

They wandered off among the tombs, stopping to read inscriptions, marvelling at the statuary, condoling with those who had died from plague or fever, sympathising with widows and victims of shipwrecks. They found the marital grave of Emma and Ebenezer Rowbridge, perfect parents mourned by their seven surviving children in 1825. Wrench invented ancestors for her, staunch non-conformists with a bible chest and a horse and buggy, good tradespeople whose younger son went to the bad.

'How?' she asked, laughing. 'What happened to him?'

'Oh, the usual . . . gambling, drink, women. He died young, in Bermuda.'

'*Bermuda?*'

'Rum-running. They didn't speak about him in front of the children. He kept a journal.'

'Really?'

'Exquisitely written, a work of genius, now mouldering in some attic.'

'In a sea-chest.'

'Exactly. Together with letters from a number of passionate married ladies and his unpaid bills.'

[87]

'All in Bermuda?'

'I'm afraid so.'

'Will it ever be discovered—the journal?'

'It might be.'

They walked on slowly. She said, 'I have this curious feeling . . . that you want to save me.'

'Save you? What on earth from?'

'I don't know. I mean . . . why do you bother with me?'

'I don't bother with you—what the hell do you mean?'

'Well . . . you think I'm wasting my time, don't you?'

'Everybody's wasting their time in one way or another.'

'No. You're getting out of it. That's not even true. It's just a sort of vague cliché, sounds vaguely profound. Why did you leave a message for me to come to the cemetery?'

'I told you. I thought you'd enjoy it.'

'I do. But why me? Why not . . . Wallace Frogmore?'

'Oh, come on . . .' He grinned broadly. 'He's not as pretty as you.'

'That's not the reason.'

'He's not as bright as you. Oh, for God's sake, why would I want to spend the afternoon in a cemetery with Wallace Frogmore?'

'It's because you think he's hopeless, and you don't think I am.'

'Well—are you?'

'From your point of view, I suppose I am.'

'And what is my point of view?'

'You told me yourself. Catholic.'

'My dear girl, Catholicism isn't a point of view, it's a way of life. You sound to me like someone yelling for help.'

'And you sound to me like someone yelling offers of help, when they're not—they may not be needed.'

'I don't think we're getting very far.'

'No. No, we're not.'

They walked on in silence, puzzling each other out. After a while he sighed, shook his head, grinned, giving up. 'You want to go to a movie tonight? It seems we've got a free evening.'

'No, I can't, Godfrey. I'm sorry.'

'The Bentley, I presume.'

'How do you know?'

'I heard. Bill Anderson saw you go out last night.'

'Then he's wrong. It was a Ferrari. Anyway, what's it got to do with Bill Anderson?'

He shrugged. 'Nothing. Bentley or Ferrari, so long as you're happy. We'll go to a movie another night.'

She wanted to take his hand and walk, swinging it, but he was untouchable. She pulled off a maple leaf and tucked it into his breast pocket, arranging it as though it were a handkerchief. He was pleased, and thanked her. They walked downhill towards the city.

$$\star \qquad \star \qquad \star$$

'He looks incapable,' Robert said, 'of an evil action.'

'Godfrey? I know. It must be a disadvantage—I mean, if he wants to be evil.'

'Well. He doesn't.' He kissed her chest, tracing every ridge and plane of bone. 'You feel anything?'

'No. But I know you're doing it, so I feel something.'

'What?'

'Pleased. Very pleased.'

'Good. That's what I want you to feel.'

'You take more notice of me there than anywhere else. You know that?'

'It's funny. I like it. It is the most innocent part of a body I have ever seen.'

'If it weren't for that . . . would I be just like anyone else?'

'Of course not.'

'But what's the difference?'

'You have no sleep, you go to the infants' school, run away from Yves Pretin, spend the afternoon in the cemetery, make love for three hours—still you're prattling.' He kissed her mouth. 'Be quiet.'

'If I'm quiet then I'll go to sleep.'

'Then go to sleep. I'll wake you.'

'No, it's a waste of time. I used to ask Ramsey . . .'

'Ramsey?'

'The . . . man I lived with. In fact, I think I've asked everyone I've ever been to bed with, and nobody will tell me.'

'What?'

'What the difference is, between one woman and another.'

'You mean, between you and other women? Well, what's the difference between this Ramsey and . . . well, me?'

[90]

'It's just a different thing altogether. But Ramsey and other men, they were quite the same, I suppose. Except that I used to love him.'

'No more?'

'What more is there?'

'No. I mean, you don't love him any longer?'

'Do you love anyone?'

'Not now . . . no, not any longer.'

'When will you tell me about it?'

'When you come back. When you've had some sleep and are bored stiff and in need of entertainment. Here, put your head down . . .'

Flora came into her sleep, pregnant and victorious; she was in an earthquake, on a sliding mountain; but she, Muriel, was laughing and laughing, as though this were the funniest thing she had ever known.

'Hey . . .'

She laughed, sleeping, into the pillow.

'Hey. Coffee. It's four o'clock.'

'When?' Wide awake, hearing the General's reveille.

In the morning. You'd better get back to the hotel.' He handed her the mug of coffee, pulled on a sweater and trousers, slippers without socks.

She smiled. 'I've never seen you look so unrespectable.'

'You've only seen me three times.'

'Four.'

'Will you have lunch with me, before you go?'

'No. I'm sorry. I'm having it with Alex MacNeish.'

He came over and held her closely. His concern and his sadness released in her a shower of love of some

[91]

kind, a small rain of tenderness and affection and gratitude. For a moment she seriously thought that she might come back for his sake, spend more time with him and hear his story.

8

'In the train on the way to Pembroke, sitting in the parlour, feeling fifteen years old, five hundred years old, the distance gallops me away. You asked what I wrote about, then said it was a silly question, and I couldn't have answered it anyway, since what I have always written about is the world as I see it from my side of my eyes, and it has never been orderly, it's never been for other people to see. Now I want you to see everything, I want to show you every minute of my life. Absurd, it's absurd, but absurdity belongs in another world, in that world I'm selfish, wicked, irresponsible, unhinged—in this I am loving and wise and even realistic in some extra-ordinary way. I feel like a rib shouting to be plucked out. Did you know this? I can't even say your name.

'It's not true that I want you to see everything.

'Quickly, anything, write anything I want you to know, write anything: we went to Italy the summer before last, Ramsey and I, we stayed in a pensione on the beach, you were in Venice. There was a beautiful brown woman on the beach, she wore a modest black swimming costume and a green cap over her long hair. She had six children under what? Under six they seemed. In the boiling rough sea, on the very edge, she used to stand with her arms akimbo, feet apart, sturdily in the centre of the tumbling children; then she would dart towards one to save its life, cuff it; chase another, smack it out of the sea; she laughed, glistened, looked worried, was obsessed. For safety, she would decide to have three in, three out. She groped in the water with her hands for slippery children. Their rubber rings, with Donald Duck and Pluto, used to be abandoned on the sand, they quivered in the wind and were sometimes airborne, lost. So she was not entirely careful.

'Keep telling you, I must keep telling you. The journalists sit in swivel chairs like a boardroom, all except Godfrey asleep, he reads a book with an expression of disgust or melancholy on his face, I can't tell which. Godfrey knows you. That has become the most important thing about him. The sea made such a row, crashing forward with a sort of exuberance, ebullience, what's the word, falling over itself, larking about, *molto periculoso*, said the guardian of the beach, and piercingly blew his whistle. I have never been to Venice, but imagine it to be full of beautiful young women and small drinks. Every day around twelve-thirty somebody stood on the rickety balcony of the beach restaurant and yelled 'Claudia!' but nobody ever seemed to come, or answer.

'You have children, you love them, play with them by the sea. I have hardly ever played with children, even when I was one. It's my past I want you to know, as though I were born to you. Every child, every young person on that beach was moving— jumping, running, throwing sand, digging heavy wet sand, pulling on fishing nets, crawling, chasing, picking out fragments of shell between finger and thumb, rolling about—except for two English girls who were absolutely lifeless, apparently near death anyway, dull, dragged down and weighted with boredom and the sun, the corners of their mouths, everything seemed to sag with some intolerable disgust. One morning I saw the brown woman close to, and she had a hard gnarled face, cunning eyes, I thought there had been an overnight coarsening.

'Then one day, one of the English girls found a boyfriend and became lively. When he dived, threading through the exact eye of the wave, she threw herself after him and seemed to disrupt half a ton of water. She was about fourteen, while she was in love she became very pretty, old ladies offered her chocolates, she talked to me sometimes. When the boy went back to Rome she played a song on the juke-box and said to me gravely, "It brings back memories."

'If only one believed in spells and incantations and potions and prayer. What am I trying to give you, and who are you, anyway? Why do I try to enchant you with an old Italian summer? I can give you twenty-six other summers, all except the last. In September groups of vulture boys appeared, all smiling, all handsome, refusing to go away or to believe they weren't wanted. There was a kind of greed and starvation everywhere. The brown woman's husband, who must have been away somewhere, began coming for the weekends; he lay all day on a lilo, flexing his muscles, eyes shut, imbibing himself. His wife started screaming incessantly, weeping easily. They seemed to have nothing to say to each other. He was incapable of relaxing, used to beat time to the juke-box on the sand, looked at his feet, smiled for no apparent reason. She gave up the children, who were taken over by a sullen girl, and when she wasn't screaming she lay like a harpooned fish for hours at a time. But one Sunday, I remember, she was happy because all her women relatives came, and they sat on the beach gossiping, she held court, they listened admiringly, they nodded and smiled. She didn't scream, she existed again. Do you understand this? The train is stopping, the journalists wake up, Godfrey folds his book and sighs, smiles at me, I've given you something and it's as useless as if I tore out the pages and threw them out of the window; but then, blown by the speed, they would be nearer to you than I am.'

$$\star \qquad \star \qquad \star$$

There was a Japanese delegation staying in the hotel, their names beautifully painted on pieces of paper pinned to their doors. Wallace Frogmore said he would never be able to stand Nips, Germans were bad enough but better than Nips. He hoped he would not be expected to eat in the dining-room surrounded by a lot of Nips. She got out of the lift on the fourth floor, leaving him to go higher, railing. In room 450 a cardboard coffin contained twelve of the largest, heaviest, most brilliantly white chrysanthemums she had ever seen: the card said 'Robert', no message or love. She put them in the bath and sat beside them, unable to make up her mind what to do, unable to use her mind for anything, simply looking hard at the white and green, tough chrysanthemums lolling in the pink bath.

There was a knock on her door and she got up and wandered towards it, opened it, expecting nothing. A bell-boy with a cable. When she saw it was from England she took it indifferently. The bell-boy hovered for a moment, then grinned at her and sprinted away down the long corridor. The cable said: DON'T AVOID FRIENDLY REDSKINS NO PRESSURE ENJOY YOURSELF TAKE CARE LOVE CLARISSA.

She was beset by love and luxury that she didn't want. The exhilaration of the lunch, the wine, the dash for the train when every red stoplight seemed to be saving her life, drained away; she only wanted to be alone, take her aching body to bed, think of him, re-explore him as though he were a secret treasure she, a child, had found in a hollow tree. Two nights without adequate sleep, of drinking whisky as though she were thirsty, two nights of strong, embittered love-making, had made her feel physically broken, as though she were old; her whole body shook, like the very old; her eyes seemed full of rheum, squinting at an indistinct reflection in the mirror. In an hour it would be time for yet another reception. She rang down to the operator and asked for the room number of Mr. Godfrey Wrench. There

[97]

was a long pause, then they said Mr. Wrench was not in the hotel.

'But he is. He's part of . . . one of our party.'

'A Japanese gentleman?'

'An English gentleman.'

'No, madam, there is no Mr. Wrench staying in the hotel.'

Her eyes filled with tears. She blinked, and the tears spilled down her face. You're only crying because you're tired, her mother said, drying her briskly with a hard white bath towel. She sat with streaming eyes in front of her father while he sat patiently fingering Neville Shute, his brown fingers eagerly transmitting drama to his tepid, gentle brain. She picked up the receiver again.

'Would you give me the room number of Miss Rowbridge, Miss Muriel Rowbridge?'

'Just a moment, please.' Another two minutes' pause. 'Miss Rowbridge checked out this morning, madam.'

'Have you any idea where she went?'

'None at all.'

'I see. Thank you.'

'You're welcome.'

She twisted round on the bed, holding the pillow. He should have given me some pills, tranquillisers, something, how dare he send me out into the world with no more than 'Take care of yourself'? Am I a responsible, whole, adult woman? The answer is yes, and you should be grateful you're not dead. She relaxed, lying very still. I'm alone. Only my body has friends. They saved it, Robert enjoys it, I throw it away. 'Cancer is an autonomous new growth of tissue of an unknown basic cause. Cancer possesses an atypical structure of the body tissues or organs in which it originates, serves no useful purpose in the economy of the individual, exhibits unlimited and uncontrolled power of growth and has the ability and tendency to spread and metastasize, or spread to distant locations where it may lodge and assume a renewal of growth. . . .' Supposing at this moment, excited by her neglect, there was a darkening and hardening in some part of her, a new corruption. Even to think such a thing was to invent it. Thoroughly frightened, she snatched the receiver again. Her voice was shaking. The same operator answered.

'Could you please give me the room number of Mr. Godfrey Wrench.'

'One moment, please . . . The number is 625. Do you wish me to connect you?'

'Yes. Yes. Thank you.'

He answered, as before, immediately. She whispered, shouting for help, 'Godfrey, I feel terrible, I just can't come to this party.'

'Then don't. It'll be just the same as all the others. What's the matter—hangover?'

'I . . . yes, I suppose so. But I'd like to see you afterwards. Couldn't we find somewhere to eat—you know, in the town?'

'I can't, love. I have to meet somebody. Why don't you get them to bring you something to your room, get some rest? From the look of it, we've got a hell of a day tomorrow.'

And be alone? But perhaps she wasn't alone.

Perhaps there was a change, after all. She said, 'All right. It's a good idea. See you tomorrow.'

He said, 'Bless you.'

*   *   *

'Here is a film for you. It lasts about one minute: In the beginning, just after he has been blinded—but she doesn't know that—she is sitting in a pram in the garden. It's sunny, there's a strong smell of wood-smoke and tar. She decides to move to the other end of the pram, but when she stands up, the pram overturns. Her father approaches down a long grass path. He is dressed in khaki with shining buttons and belt, and wears dark glasses. He doesn't appear to hurry. He walks towards her down the long grass path, presumably to the rescue.

'This is probably the first conscious plan of her life: I'll go and sit at the other end of the pram. She doesn't wait to think about it. Dressed in some sort of holland smock, bulky, shapeless and damp, she clambers up, taking a firm step in the right direction. . . .

'The aspect of life does change, but not for the better. The sky shoots past behind the beech leaves, the pram rears up, the daisies swarm, hitting her between the eyes. Flat on her stomach, she raises her big head like a boxer at the eighth count to site this long grass path, the parallel borders with their blue and fuzzy flowers stretching to infinity; and approaching, increasing, finally filling the scope of her vision, dead on, bull's-eye, at precisely the fateful moment when feeling, thought, action and fear had been discovered

[100]

—her father, dressed as a soldier, the relief of Mafeking. She waits, smug with trust.

'But he walks on. Avoiding, by some miracle, the staring child and overturned pram, its wheels turning slow as windmills, he walks on.

'He is halfway down the path before she begins to cry, then he comes back, stumbling and groping for her, shouting for her mother as he falls into the springs and spokes of the pram while she tries to crawl away from him, yelling blue murder with a broken heart. That's all there is of the story.

'I wrote it lying on my bed in room 450 of a hotel full of Japanese, the telephone tempting me to ring you. It's late, I don't know what else to tell you, I want to live all over again, exactly as I have done, but in your sight. I want you to know where the path goes after it crosses the field and how the handle of the front door is a quarter of an inch too near the lintel, I want you to make love to me when I was seventeen. In reality, of course, there's no one, you don't exist, the world is a shut skating rink with the freezing plant thundering. I sit in a high restaurant like a crow's nest, hardly touching the knee under the table, looking out at the rain and the Sacré Cœur and back at the suède forearm with beige silk cuff, amber links if I'm not mistaken—what's unfortunate about amber links, which makes me wonder whether you are a vain and stupid man? Could I ring you and ask, "Are you worth all this?" I couldn't, because you wouldn't understand. You have to be worth it.'

She broke off, shut the notebook, carefully clipped the ball-point to the cover, picked up the telephone, gave the number. Three hundred miles away, a woman answered.

'Hullo?'

'Could I speak to Mr. MacNeish, please?'

A brief pause, then, 'Who is it?'

'Muriel Rowbridge.'

'Just a moment, please.'

There was a long silence. She was not actually holding her breath, but the sensation was the same, of stifling, heart pounding. At last he was there.

'Hullo.' A slight emphasis on the 'o', surprised.

'I—I just wanted to thank you for lunch.'

'It was very pleasant. Where are you? Pembroke?'

'Yes. The hotel's full of Japanese.'

'Oh really?'

'Well . . . I just wanted to say it was a nice lunch. Maybe I'll see you at the weekend.'

'I have to go over to the Coast sometime, it might be the weekend.'

'Oh.'

'Anyway, you'll be in Pembroke for a couple of days. I'll call you.'

'All right. Goodbye.'

'Goodbye now.'

She didn't leave it there. She saw him put down the receiver, shrug his shoulders in the direction of a faceless woman lying on a sofa.

'What was all that about?' the faceless woman asked.

'Search me. This English chick I had lunch with today, calling from Pembroke of all places.'

'She's probably madly in love with you.' No. Not

that. 'The dull one at the party? What did she want?'

'Wanted to tell me her hotel's full of Japanese.'

'Oh. Well. Turn it over, darling, will you, I can't stand Victor Mature . . .'

'Could I ring you and ask, "Are you worth all this?" I couldn't, because you wouldn't understand. You have to be worth it . . .' Before she went to sleep she decided to ask the General to send her to the west coast, for further coverage.

9

AFTER the intensive efforts of the first day the organisers of the tour fell back on public buildings and monuments, bus tours of the residential areas, sightseeing. 'To see sight,' Godfrey brooded, 'would be an amazing experience.' He huddled, increasingly moody, in the corner of the bus. Occupied with her now obsessive, almost uninterrupted writing, she rarely noticed him. She had come three thousand miles to discover herself capable of two strong, conflicting experiences: sexual exuberance and intense, childlike infatuation. It was as though the excessive care of the past five months, during which time everything she felt or thought had to be therapeutic and protective, had wiped out her short adult life and started her off again in a state of innocence. She had supposed, during those five months, that she was exactly the same person that she had been before, except for a physical lack which she must learn to deal with. How to deal with it, except with vague attempts at courage and acceptance, she had no idea. Apart from her work, she had done nothing; she had seen no one but her landlady, Flora and the little boy, she had gone nowhere, cutting herself off completely from her past life. Now she began to feel a change in herself: she was becoming an unfamiliar, unpredictable woman who must, if it was to be of any use to her, re-experience the past through new eyes and new senses. If it hadn't been for that minute, almost imperceptible lump, like an inward nipple, she would still be living with Ramsey, hurrying to and from the office—half living. If it hadn't been for that, she wouldn't have come away; there would have been no reason to go to bed with Robert; there would have been no moment, empty-headed, walking downstairs, when it would have been appropriate to fall in love.

There was another change: they had told her that she was safe, that she would live to be ninety, and since normal people can live until they're ninety, she had believed them. Now, in the process of a curious metamorphosis, she began to think of dying. It seemed a natural, even probable, conclusion to this state of intense, confused feeling. It was as though she was beginning to believe that she would die on leaving this place; her return to England was as remote and certain as death. She could put it off easily enough, by going to the coast for a few days, by making love, looking at trees, drinking martinis, eating hamburgers, changing trains and hotels, writing it all down under the guardian bird on its sprig of honeysuckle; but this kind of eternity was finite, she could mark a place in her diary where it must end. As for her writing, she knew that MacNeish would never read it in her lifetime: that is, that he would never read it in her presence, or when she was in any way available. It was therefore free, truthful, illogical, written against time.

When she looked out of the window of the bus, or noticed where she was sitting, it was only to reach out and haul in some new shape, or sound, or feeling, to present to him . . .

'Robert has his tragedy, which he seems to keep hidden like the silver, an heirloom. Since—what day was it? Sunday evening?—he has been a thousandth—no, there's no small enough figure to describe it—part of what I wanted to be part of. But how can I feel so savagely, badly unfaithful to someone who has nothing to do with me? That isn't true, of course, he has more to do with me than you have, he knows me, which you will never do, he's seen me and touched me and so I feel obligated and so unfaithful, but never mind. The sun came down in great shafts after the rain and the river fog-horned forlornly, its little waves chopping under the bridges, you don't remember.

'Going up the tower of the Town Hall in the lift, the liftman said, dry and informing: "Funny thing. This morning I ran out of tower." I imagined us soaring on, silent as space, for ever. Now they've all gone up to the press gallery and because I'm a woman and feeble, and no good at my job, I sit here surrounded by portraits of jolly grey barristers, faces tight and polished as tomatoes, pretending to govern, administer, regulate what, who? For their good times they go over the river to a different section of the town. I've always been disgusted by men who make money out of people's need to be cured or saved or divorced or organised, clean the sewers or slice off the cancer or pull the children over a snotty handkerchief soaked in tears. I suppose they're necessary, but they ought to keep quiet about it. I've always been frightened of having opinions in case these sort of men (the General is one of them, exploiting some sort of need, probably loneliness) despised me. Now, for you to frame in your hands, is a file of very quiet, very neat, extremely small children, not having the faintest idea why they're here.

'In all those years of living with Ramsey, what did I tell him, what did we (pretending that you have asked me) talk about? Over a thousand days there must have been at least one conversation. He spoke a fair amount, I remember. He told anecdotes from his daily life, or from the lives of other people. He read the newspapers with great attention, but seldom discussed the news. He remarked on the weather, and was occasionally enthusiastic about some French film, although he also liked Fellini's 8½, which he saw three times. He never talked about himself in relation to me, Flora or our situation. I did, Flora did; but not Ramsey. We were therefore unable to take any kind of action, you see, since this would have meant lifting Ramsey up, transporting him, putting him down again some-where else; not just without his co-operation or against his will, but without his knowledge. And even then he would have won—I mean, kept his detachment—by not noticing the difference.

'The theory was that Flora wouldn't divorce him, and I believed this for some time, in spite of her protestations and offers of instant adultery. It took me almost two years to realise that Ramsey wouldn't *be* divorced—the idea of being without Flora was as appalling to him as the idea of being without me. The merest hint that he should make a choice—and I suppose we did a good deal more than hinting, the exasperation and frustration got too much for both of us—anyway, the faintest threat of choice and he was shattered, literally incapacitated, sometimes for days. Between us, he said, he was being eaten alive. If this was so, I don't know why we were both starving. When we first met he told me that he had been devoured for ten years. His whole idea of loving was omnivorous. Now, back with Flora, he may feel wanted again—Flora asleep, in a sleeping attitude, lashes arranged on cheeks, lips slightly parted, inviting him to slip between her pearly teeth and grope his way down into her womb. Flora is very conscious of her womb, it breathes like an octopus. There is no way into it, except to be eaten. I don't know what I was doing, trying to set him up by himself, hoping he would stand and walk and speak, the gingerbread man.

'Here they come. Bill Anderson is going to say, Scribble, scribble, scribble, eh, Miss Rowbridge? . . . He's said it.'

*   *   *

'Every time I come back to the hotel I believe there will be a message from you, I know there won't be. Why would you send a message, and what would it say? But this afternoon I saw an envelope in the pigeon-hole of 450, there was a queue to collect the keys and I felt the envelope would catch fire and burn before they gave it to me.

'The letter was from Robert and it said: "Dear M. Of Nastasya Filippovna—'there was not a trace left of her former timidity and schoolgirlish uncertainty, which had sometimes been so delightful in its unaffected playfulness and ingenuousness and sometimes so melancholy and pensive, astonished, mistrustful, tearful and restless . . . There was evidently something else here, some storm of the heart and mind, something in the nature of romantic indignation, goodness only knows why and against whom, a sort of insatiable feeling of contempt.' Write to me, if you will. R."

'I try to think what I know about you—what you read, what you like, who you are. I know practically nothing. Graham Greene and Saul Bellow, cheesecake, Bus Berkeley, herons, all those leathers. You don't like being alone, you say that being alone makes you shit-scared for some reason. You have these confusions in your life, which I suppose means women. Why does it have to be you I want, not Robert? This morning I told you about Ramsey, and I don't know why. Yesterday I knew why I was telling you everything.

'Listen, terminalia berries, eugenia bark, dandelion and logwood, heart-wood and prickly pear, guava leaves, privet, ladies' bedstraw roots and onion skins. Yesterday we went to a place where a clean woman in a folk-weave skirt was dying wool, and she thought I was writing down the recipe. I was writing down the names for love. When I reach extremes of foolishness like this it sobers me for a while, I'd like to laugh at myself but can't see the joke, I almost resent you for wasting my time.'

* * *

[109]

'I haven't seen you for days,' Godfrey said.

She laughed. 'That's not true. You see me all the time. Anyway, we haven't been here for days.'

'It seems like a lifetime. You know we haven't been inside one house? We haven't *met* anyone. Hell, we've got city councillors in Pontypool.'

'Is that where you come from?'

'Very remotely. Where shall we go?'

They looked up and down the street: parking lots, steak-'n'-chips, go-go, furniture marts, the sparse neon signs petering out in both directions into a darkness which might be the prairie or the desert but was in fact a twenty-mile sprawl of residential area.

'Depressing,' Godfrey said. 'Which way?'

'Where's downtown?'

'Here.'

'Oh well. Let's walk anyway.'

They set out. There was a cold wind, a slight spattering of rain, no comfort anywhere. She was exhilarated by this, walking rapidly, her hands in her pockets. He loped along slightly hunched, like a man who uses walking for thought. She imagined him covering Cumberland, the Highlands, the Black Forest, with this walk. She asked him and he said yes, he did walk a bit, he and his wife were fond of it. It was eleven o'clock at night and the street was empty.

'How's it going, then?' he asked.

'How's what going?'

'The writing.'

'Oh . . .' She wheeled round a lamp-post, grinning at him. 'What writing?'

'All day, as far as I can see. Everywhere.'

'Don't you do that?'

'Never.'

'No. Well. I don't know, sometimes it seems . . . urgent.'

'In what way?'

'Supposing you died . . . no one would remember.'

'Oh, come on.'

'No. I mean that. Maybe it's important, recording things. Any day, like in . . . oh, August 1964. Or now.'

'What happened in August 1964?'

'I don't know yet. But you want to know, so I might remember.'

'So what's it for? Who's going to see it?'

'I don't know. No one. Just look at that.'

She stopped in front of a bar whose neon sign blazed: 'Topless, Bottomless and Double Breasted'. 'What can it mean?' she asked.

'I don't know.'

'Shall we go in and find out?'

'No.'

'No. I suppose not.'

She walked on, leaving him to catch up, but he didn't hurry. Two men came out of an alley on the other side of the street and ran, zigzagging, across the street towards her. There was something very frightening in the silent way they ran over the empty street, one after the other who was running away. She turned quickly to find Godfrey, who was looking in a shop window. He looked up and saw her with the men.

She knew that he should come slowly, not frightening the men, but she was so frightened herself that she called 'Godfrey!'; he came very purposefully, ready to protect her, but there was no need. The middle-aged man with the hollow, haunted face wanted their protection from the young, strong one. The middle-aged one shambled very close to Muriel, running a few steps, wheeling round, muttering and shouting and pleading incomprehensibly; the young one came behind him, so close that they were almost touching. The street stretched on interminably, no one in sight. They walked in this nervous group for a few hundred yards, then suddenly the middle-aged man turned and flung out his arm wildly; the young one grabbed the arm, held it down and hit him; the older one broke away and staggered out into the street, running at random, the young one after him; at last they disappeared.

She was trembling with fear; it was like being awake in somebody else's nightmare, the urgent, useless running, the inevitable capture and horror. 'We should have done something,' Godfrey said.

'But what?'

'I don't know. Poor bloody devils.'

'Can we have a drink or something? It's silly, I'm . . .'

'Scared? So was I. Yes, of course. There's a bar over there.' He held her arm firmly and hurried her across the street. The bar was dark, with small rickety tables and a counter lined with men sitting with their backs to a four-foot makeshift stage on which a thin girl, wearily, for the fifteenth time that day, was peeling off her gloves. The music came from the radio, and as they sat down it stopped and a shrill, baby voice lisped:

'I want a pennyworth of chips.'
'Which chips, honey?'
'The noisiest chips in the world!'

The girl unzipped her dress, tugging at it rather irritably. The radio launched into the theme music from *Dr. Zhivago*. The girl threw her dress behind a screen and began to unlatch her unnecessary corset.

'We don't have to stay,' Muriel said.

'Why not? I thought you wanted a drink. Whisky?'

'Brandy.'

He asked the waitress for two brandies, and suddenly grinned at Muriel through the gloom. 'Why don't you ask me why I'm drinking?'

'Well—why are you?'

'I don't drink. But from time to time I have one. You must learn to be more tolerant.'

'Don't . . .'

'What?'

'Laugh at me.'

He patted her hand briskly and turned to look at the stage with the polite, momentary interest that he might give to a dog show on somebody else's television. The girl, with gold stars clamped over her nipples, appeared to be painting an imaginary ceiling. It was hard, monotonous work. At last, thankfully, she dropped her arms, ripped off her G-string with the relief of someone pulling off an apron, displayed a

[113]

small gold figleaf for a split second, and was gone. The music moaned on, lyrical.

When the drinks arrived he settled himself down to her. 'Well, then. What's been happening to you? What's the secret?'

She looked at him quickly. 'What secret?'

'Oh . . . the Bentley. The writing. Also there's a certain glow. Have you fallen in love, is that it?'

'Why do you want to know?'

'You don't have to tell me.'

'What do you think was the matter with those men?'

'Junkies, we couldn't have done anything. Are you happy?'

'I don't know . . . Yes, in a funny sort of way.'

'You fell for MacNeish, is that it?'

'Wouldn't you,' the radio urged, 'like to show off the prettiest complexion in town? Velvet Petal soap treats skin tenderly . . . gently . . . Velvet Petal makes you so soft to the touch . . .' A fat woman in a feather boa took the stage, the radio played the theme music from *Exodus*, she paced up and down flipping the end of the feather boa, smiling rigidly.

'Why do you think that?'

'I don't know. Just a hunch. When he brought you to the train on Tuesday . . .'

'Oh. Yes.'

'I'm right, then?'

'Look. You can't fall in love with someone you've only met twice in your life. I don't know the man. Anyway . . .' She had been playing with the swizzle-stick and suddenly it snapped in half; she dropped the

[114]

pieces on the table. 'Anyway, he's perfectly happy with his wife, and . . .'

'Well? Go on.'

'You want me to confess something, don't you?'

'Not at all. I just thought it might be easier for you if you talked about it.'

And so it would be—but not, dear Godfrey, to you. The breasts of the fat woman were immense, drooping globes, the skin on the gyrating stomach was puckered like fish-skin. Thank your lucky stars you're small, dear, it's the big-busted ones who take it hard. 'In the last six months,' she said slowly, 'I've wanted to write . . . something.'

'Then why don't you?'

'I don't know how to begin. I don't know what it would be. You see . . . I'm different . . .'

'From other people? What arrogance.'

She glanced at him, and sighed shortly. 'Everyone is different from other people. I was going to say, from the way I used to be.'

'I'm sorry. You mean, before your engagement broke up?'

She had to think before she answered. 'Yes. In a way. I suppose so.' It was impossible to tell him the truth. The truth would lay her open to more compassion than she could bear. He would, she felt, be almost triumphant. She saw the fat woman's buttocks for an instant before the merciful blackout: a huge, yellow, inverted heart hanging over her mottled thighs. The apparent impossibility of simple truth and reality began to obsess her. She wanted to shake her head furiously from side to side to rid it of dishonesties.

'Did you . . . were you very much in love?'

'I told you, we lived together for three years. I never loved anyone else. I've been alone since then. I think,' she looked at him, imploring him not to misunderstand her, 'I'll probably always be alone.'

Unhesitating, he misunderstood. 'What an absurd idea. Good God, in less than a week out here you've found at least two people to occupy yourself with . . .'

'That's not true.'

'Why are you so sorry for yourself? Dying, being alone, it's ridiculous. You're young, attractive, bright, talented—what's the matter with you?' He sounded genuinely angry. 'Christ, if you were that old hag up there, cavorting about to keep her grandchildren probably . . . The trouble with people like you is that you suffer from privileged despair. You don't know the meaning of the word.'

She held herself tightly. 'No. I expect you're right.'

'When you've looked around a bit you'll marry and have half a dozen kids, in spite of your wretched nylon.'

'Yes. Yes, I'm sure I will.'

He looked suddenly uncertain. 'I hope I'm not being stupid?'

'Of course you aren't, Godfrey. Very sensible and . . . right. Shall we go?' She was attacked, physically, with a longing for Robert, the only person in the world who knew her and accepted her entirely. Yet even this was made dishonest by the fact that she thought and felt only about someone else, a fantasy, someone she had fallen in love with in her sleep, a sickness. She wished that she had not come out this evening, but had spent it alone with her notebook; however unreal, in the notebook she at least, quite literally, made something of herself. The prospect of lifelong loneliness, which she had wanted to explain to Godfrey, terrified her. As they walked up the deserted street in silence, her isolation felt so unbearable that for the first time she regretted the swift surgery, resented what they had done to her without her knowledge.

'I've depressed you for some reason,' Godfrey said. 'I'm sorry.'

'No. I'm tired. Are you going home on Saturday?'

'Yes. Are you?'

'Yes. Yes, I think so.' Condemning herself to death.

In her room at the hotel the message eye on the telephone opened and shone in the dark.

*　　　*　　　*

She saw it immediately she went into the room, but didn't know what it was. When she had found the lights, dropped her handbag like a load on the bed, she investigated the telephone. Ring the operator, it said.

'Yes, Miss Rowbridge, there was a call for you. One moment, please.'

Robert. She didn't want to talk to him, only to be with him. She must remember to thank him for the flowers.

'Yes, Miss Rowbridge. A Mr. MacNeish called, would you ring him when you come in.'

[117]

'But,' she said stupidly, 'it's one o'clock.'

'The gentleman said he would be at this number till 2 a.m.'

'Thank you.' It's true that your knees go weak; all those things, everything, are true. 'Would you get it for me, please?'

'Surely. Just hold on.'

She held the receiver with both hands. Odd, disconnected voices calling each other over the miles, between cities. 'Your number is ringing now.'

Don't answer it, she implored; don't be there.

But he answered, brusquely, 'Hullo?'

'This is . . .'

'Oh—Muriel. Hi. How are you?'

'I'm fine.' Her voice, if it could be seen, would be at the wrong end of a telescope, a faint insect voice. 'How are you?'

'Fine. Tired. We're starting the music, Friday.'

'Oh.' There was no other possible comment. 'Are you . . . going to the Coast?'

'Next week maybe. Look, I've got to come up to St. Andrews tomorrow, we're looking at a couple of locations. You want to have lunch?'

'Yes.'

'Now come on . . . are you going to be there?'

'We . . . they . . . don't go till the afternoon. I'll come earlier.'

'Make it dinner. You know where you're staying? Well, it's bound to be the Excelsior. I'll see you in the lobby about eight, okay?'

'Yes,' she said. 'The Excelsior at eight.'

'Take care, then. Hey, by tomorrow I meant today.'

[118]

'I know,' she said.

'All right, then. Eight this evening. 'Bye now.'

'Goodbye.'

She put down the receiver as though it were extremely fragile. Then suddenly, her knees weak, heart thumping, throat dry, she hugged herself with delight. It's all true—feeling, keeling, reeling, love not above, moon without June, eyes like stars, romancing dancing . . . General, dear General, you're on to a *good thing*, why couldn't I see it? She saw two knobs in the bedside table and turned one, longing for an explosion, to fuse all the lights, to feel herself ejected out of the room into the cold night: since it was a radio, music flooded out. Holding herself, smiling with a downward, closed smile, she danced across the room. The wall mirror met her coldly. She looked at herself like a child who has been caught stealing. Her clasped arms pushed out her breasts; she dropped her arms to her sides. Suddenly, without warning herself, she began to cry. She beat her fists on the glass table-top, and cried.

10

'I̲ɴ ᴛʜᴇ bus I want to write something for you, a present to bring you, poetry or some small object of writing that you could keep around the place. It's flat, flat, only the sky is curved, the lake silver, the Ford Motor Company, Bomac Steel, parking lots and parking lots crammed with glinting cars, Beechville pop. 51,000, the double track highways so narrow that when the bus passes a car it almost drives on the kerb: Kraft Cheese Whiz, Live Royally— Start your mink-for-her savings now! Eighty miles of nothing, but going towards you for—I don't know what purpose.

'Everyone is dead silent this morning, Bill Anderson and Wally Frogmore and the boys, no jokes. They haven't found any girls and the trip is almost over, all their wives are re-emerging from Haywards Heath and Norbury and Esher, only the wives can make them feel like men again. Try hard, now; I'm going to try.

'There were nights, some nights, when she would wake after some dream and begin to think about him, always with the conscious knowledge that this would be painful. How long can a longing last, she didn't know. Only the foolishness of it humiliated her. Like

[120]

a child (but why like a child?) she planned how they would meet, what she would say; how they would come together like two people who had been forcibly kept apart for oh God, such an intolerable time. Then, and it was always at night, she felt that he was the only person she loved, the only person alive to whom she wanted to say I love you, and follow, and be with, and obey and honour.

'Knowing the whole time that this was a lie, because such a thing was a monstrous fantasy. But the real, the physically felt love in her could be conjured up simply by thinking of him standing somewhere, doing anything; the need in itself was real. At the hopelessness of satisfying it she cried, beat with her fists, and felt so alone that the presence of anyone else was a kind of abuse. At the same time it seemed that the only thing to do was to occupy herself with someone else, it hardly mattered who . . .'

She snapped the book shut, defeated. At the same time and on the other hand, looked at in one way and then again, looked at in another—wandering in a wilderness of feeling where one way was as good as another, since there was no future to move towards and no past to rely on.

'I can't . . . I mean, there isn't any choice any more. So it's pointless. You have to go back to Flora.'

'Back to Flora?'

'Or live by yourself. I don't know.'

'I don't want to live by myself. I want to live with you.'

'No, you don't. I'm sorry. Yes, you do, but you just want things to be the same and they aren't the same.

You couldn't ever make yourself choose. Now it's impossible, don't you see? I just feel . . . you're sorry for me, there isn't any real choice any more.'

'I'm so confused . . . I'm not sorry for you, anyway. You're just the same to me as you always were.'

'That's not true.'

'No, it's not. But we could work something out, couldn't we? I mean, we don't have to take all these mad decisions all of a sudden? I can't leave you, anyway. I'd feel a bastard.'

'Ramsey, please, please take me seriously.'

'You mean you don't love me any more?'

'You can't see, can you? You're blind.'

'Well, that's a fine thing to say . . .'

'I don't know if I love you. Yes, I love you. Maybe I always will, but it doesn't make any difference. I just want you to go. Please. Before I come out of here. Please, Ramsey.'

'I shall have to talk to Flora. Maybe she won't want me back. She's got used to being on her own. Oh, darling, my darling, it's all bloody silly nonsense, you don't really want me to go. I mean, I don't give a damn whether you've got one tit or two, why do we have to have all this drama?'

But he did care. He would never have touched her again without an effort that would have worn him out. He was, in any case, fairly apathetic about sex, much preferring fantasy to reality. In the past she could enter his fantasy, dress up, lark about, play games. For both of them this would now be intolerably ghoulish. If he had been capable of including her, she might not have shut herself out; but there it was, a one-way insuperable barrier against which they could mourn for the rest of their lives, but never again touch. This was the need she felt could never be satisfied, the sense of forced separation, the wilderness in which one way was as pointless as another, since none of them led through the barrier, and home. Robert had been a place to stay the night, and she couldn't believe that he would ever become more than that. She was going to MacNeish with all the timorousness and hope of someone who sees an oasis in a land of mirages. Even while she was sitting in the bus thinking painfully of Ramsey, she didn't realise that the oasis had the familiar look of the barrier; that she was still crying to be identified, recognised and taken in.

*   *   *

St. Andrews was an hilarious surprise. It was a town built of water, water crashing down from the wide, rapidly flowing rivers above into whirlpools and lakes and grottoes below, the houses perpetually soaked, one drank as one breathed. Demented gulls, driven mad by the incessant tempest, blew through the spray like so many single feathers, tossed up and back, falling, rising again with no need to beat their wings.

'It's like a Victorian oleograph,' Godfrey said. 'Nature In The Raw.' He looked pleased, happier than he had done for days. The others, with heaven knows what memories of forbidden wetness, buckets and hoses, water-shoots, water-pistols, falling in and throwing the stuff about, became foolish as boys, which suited them. It was only four o'clock, and she was glad to go with them to the caves, the boats, all the watery fun they could find. Wallace Frogmore said, 'Left your notebook behind, dear? The General *will* be glad.' She didn't care.

The mouths of the caves were solidly blocked with falling water. Dressed from head to foot in black oilskin like a bevy of drunken monks, they hallooed and sang and ran towards the water waving their arms as though to frighten it away, then staggered back laughing. After this they charged down the slippery path to the boat, a modest little paddle steamer that hourly chugged within daring distance of the great waterfall, flipped its stern at it and scurried back. The most dour and dignified of them had become childlike, their faces broken into huge wet smiles. As they were all identically clothed, there was no way of recognising anyone. She edged up to the front of the boat, squeezing in between two unidentifiable figures. Her oilskin hood bothered her, she wanted to douse her head in the whirling water, to be drenched all over. She pulled off the hood, shaking her hair loose, and in a moment was sleek as a dog, gasping.

'Hullo, there.'

Her eyes were full of water, water running into her mouth. She looked up and peered at the man beside her.

'It's you.'

'I thought you weren't arriving till later.'

'We've only just got here—I mean, not long . . .'

'Is that good for your hair, do you think?'

'I . . . don't know!'

He laughed. 'It's nice to see you, anyway.'

'It's nice to see you too.'

'What do you think of it?'

She couldn't think of a word. 'Fantastic.'

'Can you imagine what the first Indian thought—the first one who ever saw it, padding along up there in the woods? First the noise. Then, bam, the place itself. They didn't distinguish between people and things, this must have been the most almighty person.'

'Well . . . God.'

'Oh, sure, it must have been a god. And it's taken a lot of sacrifices, too, in its time. You know it keeps a body for four days exactly before spewing it up on the bank there?'

'Are you going to make a film here?'

'We may use it.'

The boat, having touched the spray with its nose, turned skittishly; she stumbled against him and he put his arm round her, steadying her. The oilskin was like armour, she couldn't feel anything but the weight of his arm, and she herself was safe within layers of armour. She smiled at him. He flipped at her drowned hair.

'What are you going to do with it?'

'Nothing.'

'Just let it dry?'

'Yes.'

'I see.'

His blue, close-set eyes looked at her thoughtfully for a moment from the depths of his hood. 'You're a funny girl.'

She questioned him.

'We're taking a helicopter over here tonight. You want to come?'

'Yes, I'd love to.'

'And we're having dinner, is that right?'

'Yes.'

'Good. I'll see you, then.' He left her. When she turned round, she couldn't recognise him; but he and two other men were first off the boat and climbed the path in a group, talking earnestly together.

'Wasn't that MacNeish?' Godfrey asked, catching up with her.

'Yes. He's looking at locations.'

'Did you know he was going to be here?'

He seemed like a kind of voyeur, but he was apparently totally unaware of it. She said shortly, 'Yes. He rang me last night.'

'You didn't tell me.'

She tried to be patient. 'After we came back.'

'Really? That was very late.'

'Yes,' she said, 'it was very late.'

She wanted desperately to be alone. Godfrey followed her like a dogged child, not letting her out of his sight. He was full of unspoken questions. She shook him off, at last, in the hotel lobby and ran for her room. The windows were misty with water, the room was like the deck of a liner, high and light and drenched in spray. She flung herself down on the bed with a great sigh and stretch of relief.

So that's him. That's the man I've been talking to, longing for. 'And it's taken a lot of sacrifices, too, in its time . . .' Oh, do you know what I feel, do you know what I want, do you know how impossible it

[126]

is? 'You're a funny girl.' Well, supposing I were a dying woman? He wouldn't want to know. That terrible phrase of complete indifference: he wouldn't want to know. Keep your secrets to yourself, honey, please. He would never say that, of course; but I hear him say it. Let's not go into all that, let's not have any dramas.

She knew that the voices in her head were telling the truth, but she could choose not to listen to them. Her hair was drying, soft and straight; she sat up and brushed it carefully.

*   *   *

'It's a funny thing,' he said, 'how easily I talk to you, I felt it right away at that party—you know I was really disappointed when you couldn't come back, though the moment I'd asked you I knew it wouldn't work really. Life's too complicated—you know? Joss is a marvellous woman, I adore her, but if I'd taken you back she would have . . . Oh, I don't know, jumped to the wrong conclusions. You know, I'm forty years old and I still don't understand women. Joss is an actress, a bloody fine actress incidentally. She goes about the world, it's not as though she were stuck at home with the kids and nothing to think about. But I'm her life, that's all there is to it. I can't do a damn thing without hurting her and I don't *want* to hurt her, it's the last thing I want to do. Well, maybe it'd be easier if she didn't work, maybe it'd be easier if she didn't do so much work with me, anyway. You know, you don't get any break. That night when you rang, I couldn't talk, you must have thought me pretty rude—anyway, she wanted to know who you were, why you were ringing, it wasn't at all easy. I think by the time you're forty you want a few things easy, I know I do. It's complicated . . . Joss is my age, of course she's a remarkably beautiful woman, in fact she's more beautiful now than she ever was, but she had the kids rather late in life—well, she was thirty-four with the first one, that's not exactly rushing it—and she doesn't want anything to change, not until they're older anyway, I suppose she might take a bit of change when they're out of the way. But hell, you know, they're only four and six. That's a long time to go. You get to feel . . . your life's running out. You don't mind me talking to you like this, do you? . . . Look, the thing is really, of course, there's this bloody girl pestering me out of my mind. I suppose that's not quite honest—you can tell, can't you? I don't exactly discourage her. In fact, I suppose I'm quite fond of her, that is when I'm not hating her guts. You know, she's just a script girl, nothing— marriage broke up and she's got a small kid to support, I tried to help her and one thing led to another, now she's been round my neck for two years. No, I'm not being honest. I'm trying to make you sorry for me and that's not right. Evie's a splendid girl, and she puts up with a lot from me, but what the hell more can I give her? You know, what I want is one thing . . . peace. Just a small area of peace and quiet. It's like being a kid again, you know? Surrounded by parents and schoolteachers and God knows what. I simply want to be able to take who I like to dinner, like I'm taking you now, and go where I want and not have to answer questions the whole time. Sure, this only applies to women, but the bloody world's full of women, especially in my business—absolute dolls most of them, all throwing themselves at your head— you know, the mighty director and all that. Maybe it'd be simpler if I switched. You know, I don't think she'd mind that? Joss, I mean. God, I could have an affair with anything that wasn't a woman. But women: her territory. Keep Out. By invitation only. You know what I mean? . . . Hell, I suppose I sound bitter to you. And I'm not. I just can't keep the rules, that's all. Joss's rules. I love her. I'm mad about the kids. But I just can't keep the bloody rules all the time.

'Well, what are you thinking about, funny Muriel? Your hair looks very pretty. Soft. That's the sort of thing Joss might do, but Evie, never. You're very much like Joss in many ways. Younger, of course. She used to be a scatty sort of girl, she had absolutely no patience. I suppose patience comes with having kids, or maybe living with someone like me. What do you think? You're not going to write all this down, are you? I should know better than to talk to journalists. No. I trust you. That's the funny thing, I trust you completely. Funny little drowned rat you looked on the boat . . . You've got hands like a mole, too, a drowned mole—no, really, look, brown with the pointed fingers. You want a ride in that helicopter? I said we'd meet Gerry at nine-thirty, so we'd better be going.'

★   ★   ★

She sat between MacNeish and the man Gerry, flying in a bubble over the floodlit water. MacNeish's arm was round her. It should have been one of the happiest times of her life. The water played about in the lights like a giant fountain, fed by the dark rapids above. Lights winked, streamed, arced in the watery air, the solid earth had become a reflection in water. They hovered up here in the dry.

MacNeish gave her shoulders a little squeeze. 'Like it?'

She nodded.

'You're very silent. Happy?'

She nodded again, keeping her arms tightly to her sides.

'Take her back the other side, Gerry. It looks like a great deal of nothing to me.'

Gerry put the helicopter into a 'U' turn; they bounced back on the other side of the river.

'Is anything the matter?'

'No, of course not. I'm just a bit cold.'

'We'll have a brandy when we get back, warm you up.'

In spite of his apparent concern she knew, absolutely certainly, that she didn't exist for him. It was because she didn't exist for him that he had idly asked her to dinner, and that she was now flying with him, like a realised dream. Because she didn't exist he might even suggest, later, that they made love. This didn't, unfortunately, make her angry: it stopped her existing. She couldn't feel herself, or the warmth of his arm, she couldn't speak, she didn't think, she was an object. Look at me, she wanted to shout, look at me. His eyes glanced over her, kindly, even affectionate.

He said, behind her head, to Gerry, 'I saw Marty's chick yesterday—you know, the new blonde? She wants to do a test.'

'You have to be joking,' Gerry said. 'With a staple in her navel?'

'She can't help the way she looks. I think she's got talent.'

'Man,' Gerry said, grinning peacefully, 'she's got two talents.'

'This is a fantastic girl,' MacNeish explained patiently, 'you've never seen such a figure in your life . . .'

She murmured something like, 'Really?'

'Or such a lot of it,' Gerry said. 'Those bristols should be insured for a million dollars.'

'She's really a bright girl, a very bright girl, only because of this extraordinary appearance she just can't get a break. Everyone just roars with laughter when she says she doesn't want to strip. Seriously, though, it's tough.'

'So she should have an operation,' Gerry said.

'Oh hell. She needs something to fall back on.'

'She's got that too, if I remember.'

They laughed. She knew it was a harmless conversation between two harmless men, nothing to do with her. She wanted to escape before her mistake became too obvious, while she could still fool herself a little; but the determination to prove that she wasn't mistaken was stronger. Supposing she told him that she had fallen in love? He wouldn't want to know why. He would be flattered, not at all surprised; maybe even magnanimous. Anyone with any pride would say thank you for the ride, it was very interesting, I'm tired now, so good night. Anyone with any pride would have left Ramsey long before it became inevitable. Children without pride do anything to make themselves noticed; the nearest they get to understanding blindness is to stagger about with their eyes screwed tight, blundering into things.

Gerry brought the helicopter down on to the empty, arc-lit field. She climbed out and ran under the whirring propeller, across the field. MacNeish caught her up and took her right arm. She pretended to have something in her shoe, took it off and shook it, gave him her left arm. He hurried her to the car. As they drove away he said, 'You haven't spoken for hours. Or maybe I just haven't heard you?'

She laughed, sounding indifferent. 'I'm sorry. I don't talk much, anyway.'

'You talked at lunch the other day.'

'Well. I was nervous. I didn't know you.'

'So you only talk to people you don't know? That's funny.'

She didn't say anything.

'I like quiet women, anyway. Joss even talks in her sleep.'

'And Evie?'

'Oh, Evie . . . Yes, I guess she talks. But I don't really listen. That's terrible, isn't it?'

'Well . . . I don't know.'

'You're a very good listener.'

'Am I?' she asked dryly.

'Yes.'

[132]

As he drove, he put his right hand on her thigh. It might have been a dog's neck he was resting his hand on. She closed her eyes and clenched her teeth; if she could, she would have stopped up her ears to prevent the longing coming out. Her reason, her experience, her most ancient memory, all warned her to give up now. She made a slight effort as they went into the hotel.

'Well. Thank you very much, it was . . .'

'Let's have brandy up in my room. It's a bloody great suite, in fact, so you'll be perfectly safe.'

'I wasn't worrying,' she said, 'about being safe. But the bar's just here.'

'They won't let you in in trousers.'

'I could put a skirt on.'

'Oh, come on. I've got three settees, four armchairs, two hideous sideboards and a bidet. We'll look at television if you like.'

She looked as though she were smiling, but she was full of fear. As they walked towards the lift, Godfrey came across the lobby—to the rescue? He smiled at them, made a vague gesture and hurried on.

'Who's that?' MacNeish asked.

'Godfrey Wrench. You met him at that party. He's a great admirer of yours, perhaps we should . . .'

He wasn't listening. The lift doors slid open, they went up twenty floors as though shot from a gun. His suite was a penthouse, glass-walled, looking down on the torrential water.

'I don't know why you needed a helicopter.' Rather than an observation, it was a phrase: where is the nearest undertaker? show me to the slaughterhouse, do you have a nun's habit, size twelve?

He poured the brandy, discovered there was no ice, debated whether to call for some, decided against it. She watched him move about the room; there was a physical pain in watching him and knowing that the barrier was there, impossible to break down. At last he came and sat beside her, sighing, stretching out.

'Well, then. Tell me something.'

'What?'

'Oh, I don't know . . . What you're writing about.'

'That's . . . impossible.'

'I imagine it's very poetical and obscure and I shouldn't understand a word of it. Am I right?'

'I don't know.'

'You're very tense. Come on, relax . . .' He pulled her gently towards him; she leant against him like a wooden doll, her head on his shoulder, her eyes, since he couldn't see them, tight shut. His hand stroked her left shoulder, moved the skin over her collar bone; with his thumb on her collar bone, his fingers moved down to the rise of her breast. She wanted to cry out, to hide her face in him and shout. He was talking, as his fingers moved up and down. She couldn't believe it. 'It's funny, I feel badly about the way I talked to you about Evie. I guess I was just showing off, trying to make out I'm a good deal tougher than I really am. Why do people do that? I mean, the truth is that I'm very dependent on Evie. She's not very bright but, you know, she's simple, I can relax with her. I've had a hell of a hard time with Joss one way and another. Did I tell you how she wrote herself this anonymous letter?'

She shook her head slightly. Once upon a time, she

began to tell herself, there was a scorpion who wanted to cross the river . . .

'God, it was frightful, about six months ago—last May. Joss began to suspect something, so she put private detectives on to me and, of course, discovered the whole bit about Evie. She knew this was a bloody awful thing to do, and she couldn't admit having done it—I'd have left her right away at that point, in spite of the kids—but she couldn't bear me not knowing that she knew, you understand?'

She nodded. The scorpion said, 'It's you who's crazy. If I stung you, I'd drown,' so the frog agreed to take him across the river . . .

'So she writes herself this anonymous letter, with every single detail in it that she'd discovered from the detectives. Of course, I didn't know she'd written it. Boy, what an actress! She came dashing to the studio one morning, white as a sheet, and showed me this thing. I couldn't even swear she was acting. She was sick, do you know, physically sick? So I feel absolutely terrible and there's a week of bloody hell, and I give up Evie for ever, and the kids are all dragged into it— Jesus, what a drama! Then in the summer we go to Europe and we're staying in this hotel in Seville and one night she says to me, cool as a cucumber, that she wrote the letter and would I like a divorce. What can you do with a woman like that?'

She moved her head a little. His fingers kept stroking. 'Why?' the frog asked, 'why?' and the scorpion said, 'Because it is my nature.'

'I gave up. Well, I didn't want a divorce, what with the kids and everything. Anyway, you know for a

[135]

man in my position to be unmarried—it's murder. Evie would have expected me to marry her, and that would really have driven me crazy. I'm better off with Joss, even if she is a bit nutty at times.'

'She'll end up putting a knife in your back.'

'Are you sympathising with me, or identifying with her?'

She sat up, moving away from him. 'A bit of both . . . I must go to bed now. It's our last day tomorrow.'

'Are you coming back to town?'

'I don't know.' She looked at him with cool despair. 'Maybe I should go straight back to London. I don't know.'

'If you're coming back, I'd like to take you to the studios—it might be interesting for you. Why don't we have lunch on Saturday, then I'll take you down in the afternoon?'

She got up, folding her arms over her breast, holding her arms tightly, and walked across the huge room. She stood by the glass wall looking down at the water; his reflection came towards her in the glass; he turned her round, as though she were on a pivot, and kissed her slowly, searching her mouth. She longed to hold him, but her arms remained clasped like a shield.

'God,' he said, 'you're tense! Maybe I made the most godawful mistake.'

'No. No. You didn't make a mistake.'

'What's the matter, then? What's the trouble?' He unlocked her arms deliberately, as he might unfasten her clothes.

'Nothing. Nothing's the matter . . .'

[136]

'You're not a virgin, are you? No, I know you're not. Have you got the curse—because I don't give a damn about that, in fact I rather like it . . .'

She stared at him. He was honest. He knew that she wanted him—why refuse the gift? She couldn't think of a lie, and she couldn't tell him the truth. She said, 'I'd like to come to the studios.'

'That's not the point,' he said tartly. His vanity was disturbing him, he was beginning to think that he had made a fool of himself.

'Yes, it is.' Meaningless, but he might puzzle for some meaning in it.

'You're saying you don't know me well enough? Oh, come on. You'll never know me any better . . .'

'Are you going to the Coast next week?'

He looked alert, wary. 'Why? Do you want to come?'

'I don't know. I mean, if it was easy . . .' She ended up in a rush: 'We could think about it?'

He was already thinking about it. 'Yes,' he said. 'We could. You want another drink?'

'No, thank you.' He had left her, was far away on the other side of the room, pouring himself a brandy. She said, 'Alex . . .' the first time she had used his name. He came back to her, holding his glass. With his free hand he held her face up, as though it were a mirror. His voice was quite gentle. 'Look, honey, I don't know what your complications are—but I can't be doing with them. I've got enough of my own. Understand?'

She nodded, tears rushing to her eyes, hating herself.

'If it was all going to be simple—fine. You interest me a lot. That's the trouble. It's always the complicated ones who do interest me. But there's obviously something bothering you. So let's forget it.'

Her whole instinct was to burst into tears and run away. She was exhausted by pretending. She smiled, and put her mouth against his cheek, not kissing him. 'All right. We'll forget it. I'd still like to see the studios.'

'Sure. What plane will you take?'

She had prepared herself for this, anyway. 'There's one that gets in at twelve-thirty.' She was bold now, daring him to escape her. 'Will you meet me?'

'Okay. If you want me to.' He grinned, congratulating her on her recovery. 'Don't eat on the plane. We'll go somewhere.'

'All right.'

He came with her to the door and gave her a brief, affectionate kiss. All the longing and feeling of the past few days broke loose, she was clinging to him, feeling the back of his neck, his chest, his shoulders, finding his mouth again and again. But even now she avoided his hands with the skill of a bull-fighter, moving and shifting her body, finally enraging him so that he grabbed her without any pretence of tenderness, and found her breast.

She pushed him away with all her strength. He stared at her for a minute, shrugged. 'I'm sorry.'

'I'll explain. On Saturday.' She was pleading with him again.

'If you like.'

'I'll see you at twelve-thirty?'

He made a mock bow, hand to his forehead. Before she had gone five paces down the corridor she heard the door close.

11

T HE next morning there was a cable from the General: IF COAST REALLY NECESSARY FOR YOU OR US OF COURSE GO STOP ARE FUNDS HOLDING OUT STOP CALL ME COLLECT SATURDAY WITH PLANS LOVE CLARISSA. There was also a letter from Robert: 'M. Et même si j'essayais de dire en français ce que l'anglais refuse de me laisser exprimer, serais je plus avancé; j'en doute; car ce n'est pas tellement l'essence mais l'existence même de certains états, de certains reflets, de moments, que je me sens incapable d'exprimer . . . Ce qui est peut-être le plus important, et je le réalise à cet instant, c'est qu'ayant échangé si peu de mots, nous soyons, par quelque modeste magic, devenus si proches que le langage même, inventé sur nos lèvres, apparait superflu. Where are you, where *are* you? I am here. R.'

She threw down the cable, but held the letter for a long time, sad and grateful, almost as though she had discovered it after his death. She scrawled on a sheet of hotel writing paper: 'Robert, I'm here too, but I'm coming back. Will ring you tomorrow—maybe we can take the boat in?' She didn't believe this, but wanted to give him something, even if it turned out to be a lie. Then she telephoned the hotel where she had stayed before, and booked a room.

'We only have doubles, madam. Shower or bath?'

'Bath.'

'Twin or kingsize?'

'Beds, you mean?' She hesitated in front of the word. 'Kingsize, I think.'

She would tell him, of course—nothing else to be done. He didn't like complications, and she would make it very simple. There it is, take me or leave me. By then he would have no alternative, he would have to take her. Before she dressed she looked at herself carefully in the mirror, at the white, taut skin that no one but Robert had ever touched. At the very least, she thought harshly, it makes a change. She had a sudden doubt about her clothes, a longing to swell under frills and ribbons—'Brighten up your formal gowns with a garland of flowers or a lush corsage. If you are the sophisticated type, adopt the always fashionable Grecian lines . . . A part bow or a contrasting built-up neckline will create an "original" from last year's cocktail dress . . .' But nothing you do will turn you into Marty's chick, staple your navel, fold you up among those double-breasted, silicone-extended bunnies who threaten the well-being of Joss and Evie. Needing reassurance, knowing she wouldn't get it, she rang his room. He had already left. She tried to read through what she had written over the past few days, but it bewildered her. Terminalia berries, heart-wood and prickly pear, the names for love? Poetical and obscure, I shouldn't understand a word of it. Here's a film for you, it only lasts one minute. Who was she writing to? Before she fully understood she had taken him old flowers and stones, a pair of doll's eyes, a bit of bone to look at. The things he could never feel were the words she wrote, and after a few attempts to read them out loud, when they became exposed and awkward, she gave up. If she was untouchable, if words were all she had, what was to be done? She couldn't exist for him.

They took the bus back to the city, the journalists loaded with souvenirs made in Denmark, Japan and England. She was sorry to leave the water. It had been the one place she found possible to believe in. Godfrey came and sat beside her and she wondered whether he always made people feel that they were treating him badly, or whether it was her guilt at having behaved badly.

'Did you have a good time last night?'

'What do you want me to say—yes or no?'

He was startled. 'I'm sorry. It seemed a reasonable question.'

'If I say yes, you'll disapprove of me. If I say no then presumably I'm not very happy. I think you'd prefer that.'

'My dear girl, you're crazy. What's got into you?'

'I'm indulging,' she said, 'in a moment of privileged despair.'

He drew his breath sharply, as though in pain, and slammed open a newspaper. She had antagonised him at last, and she was sorry. There seemed nothing else to do. She couldn't write any more. The bus rattled over the flat country.

At last he said, 'I hear you may go to the Coast next week.'

'How on earth did you hear that?'

'I don't know. I think Frogmore told me.'

'But how did he know?'

'Search me. Anyway, are you?'

'I don't know . . . I might.'

'For business or pleasure?'

'I can't afford to go for pleasure.'

'So Lady Clarissa will be paying? Don't you think that's a bit unethical?'

'She doesn't seem to.'

He shrugged his shoulders slightly. 'You're lucky.'

'Yes. I am. But if you had the chance . . . would you go?'

'Probably not.'

'Why?'

'There wouldn't be any point. Besides, I'm sick of trailing about hotels. I want to get home.'

'But I don't. I don't ever want to go home.'

She said it with such childish passion that he smiled. 'You'd just like to drift, for ever?'

'I don't know about for ever. For now—that's what's important.'

The Japanese had left the hotel, it was grey and raining in the city, they had seen everything and were discontented. She sat on her bed in room 450 and stared at the gritty rain in such an intense state of waiting that everything about her—heart, blood, hunger, thirst, thought and feeling—seemed suspended; she could sit here until tomorrow morning without moving a muscle or blinking her eyes, until

[142]

it was time to go. But when the telephone rang she moved like lightning, falling over herself in her anxiety to reach it, capturing it with both hands as though it might dart away.

'Yes? Yes?'

'Wally here, Muriel. Look, the boys and I thought we might have a bit of a get together tonight, seeing we're all off home tomorrow. Well, most of us are off home. You're staying, I understand.'

'What a good idea,' she said drably. 'Yes, I am.'

'Some of them want to see these psycho-wajjer-macallit films and have a bite to eat and go to a couple of clubs after. How does that sound to you?'

'Fine,' she said.

'Good. We're sorry not to have seen more of you on this trip, but you've been such a busy girl, eh? We'll meet in the lobby, then, about eight.'

'Fine,' she said. 'Thank you.' She was going to haul herself forward again, across time.

*   *   *

Bus. Yellow, single-decker. The experience of bus. Bus sideways, backwards, frontwards, top of bus, bus upside down. Bus from a distance, interior of bus, essence and subsistence and becoming and actualisation of bus. Meaning of bus? Bus. Yellow, single-decker, etc., etc., etc. The sound-track made the fairly conventional noise which normally is trapped inside a child's transistor radio; accompanying the bus experience, it was destructive to the fragile apparatus of hearing. The journalists guffawed a little, some screwing up their eyes against the pain.

Somebody said sourly, 'Why didn't we go to the strip show?'

Godfrey said, 'I find it a little difficult to understand.'

Man with beard. Plain girl eating pomegranate. Legs in trousers. Boy rolling a marijuana cigarette (laughter). Plain girl eating. Man with beard. Man up a tree. Legs in trousers. Boy smoking cigarette (laughter). Man up a tree. The experience of non-experience, essence of nonentity, actuality of blank.

'It's a religious experience,' she said mildly.

Godfrey rolled his eyes in the gloom.

'Who's for the strip show?'

'Wait a minute,' a cautious whisper. 'We don't want to offend them.'

'We couldn't,' Godfrey said, 'offend them.'

'Tonight we relive in reverence . . . the illumination of the Buddha. When they say he's the Prince they mean he's a well-brought-up boy who went to college. He had a thousand dancing girls, or a television set. They kept him from the discovery that there was a way of turning on—of solving the riddle of sickness, age or death. "What are you doing? Sitting around waiting for the death bell to ring?" So the Buddha dropped out of school and quit his job and set out on the internal voyage looking for a man who would turn him on . . . Focus on centre. Centre. Drift within. Drift to the centre. "Help, help, I'm bleeding to death." Bleed to death. Return to the source. Flesh of my flesh, soul of my soul, we are all one. So the Buddha came down and, in whatever media they had in those days, he called a press conference. "Tune in, turn on, and before you know it you'll have dropped out." And people are saying, "Look at him, he left his wife and children, he went to the hills, and he seems very happy. . . ." This mystery is going on tonight in thousands of rooms in this city. You have to be out of your mind to pray. You have to be a flipped-out psychotic. If you know how to pray, you'll never have a bad trip, you'll never have a nervous breakdown. Each of you is the Buddha. Did you forget that? Did you get so involved in the twentieth century that they made you forget who you are . . . ?'

A hellish group burst into an anthem more or less about a green snake that was seven miles long. Apart from the journalists, the meagre audience sat impassive, dropped out beyond recall.

'We're off!' Wally hissed. They filed out rubbing their sensible heads, exhaling great sighs of relief.

'It's tragic,' Godfrey said, severely shaken. 'Tragic!'

She wanted to say, But everything is tragic. Instead, to comfort him, she took his arm. He didn't appear to notice, but walked up the street with great strides, breathing a clean wind.

*   *   *

On four single pedestals four single people, two boys and two girls, jigged like performing bears. The pedestals were not white-hot, there were no scourges and no apparent reason for it. The evening had been disaster. As the only woman she had felt for a few moments, after the psychedelic films, a hopeless sense of responsibility, but she had soon given up. It was all beyond them, the brazen din of the beat groups, the pallid novitiate girls, the apathy, the wild gyrations, the Coca-Cola and root beer.

'God,' someone groaned, 'to get back to civilisation!'

'I'll settle for Bexley Heath.'

They were disgusted with themselves for not having had a good time, they couldn't look each other in the eye, each one of them knew that the others were pretty tame fellows when it came down to it. They drifted back to the hotel through the drizzling rain, no longer trying to communicate with each other. There was a slight flare-up of bonhomie in the lobby, when those who were leaving the next day said good-bye to those who were staying, or going elsewhere. Some even suggested meeting in London, but the evening would obviously always stand between them. Muriel shook hands with them all, aware that as far as they were concerned she had not joined it, she had wandered off into a fit of acute Virginia Woolfism, she was a misfit and a failure. They smiled at each other more warmly than they had ever done before and murmured good luck, *bon voyage*, take care. She looked for Godfrey, but he had disappeared. Going up in the lift by herself she felt a moment of regret, as though she were leaving school and hadn't made the best of it.

She had not unpacked properly for days. In a burst of impatience and energy she turned both her suitcases upside down on the bed and began to sort out the mess, starting again from the beginning. She was not letting herself think about tomorrow; every time the anticipation, excitement, nervousness began she deliberately switched it off and tried to think about something else. However, when there was a knock on the door it didn't occur to her that it could be anything but a message cancelling their meeting; during the long walk to the door she had already given up hope, returned to London, let herself into the dusty, empty flat on an English Sunday morning . . .

'Hullo,' Godfrey said. 'I've come to talk to you.'

She was pleased. 'There's nowhere to sit. Wait a minute.' She took an armful of clothes and dumped them back in the suitcase.

'And brandy. I thought we needed it after this evening.'

'A week ago you only drank orange juice.'

'Well. There you are.' He poured brandy into two glasses, gave her one and sat down on the bed. 'I suppose it's silly. I just didn't want us to part on bad terms.'

'We aren't on bad terms.'

'Well. Cheers. I didn't feel we were exactly . . . communicating.'

'If you felt that,' she said embarrassed, 'it was probably my fault.'

'Oh, I don't think so. I can be extremely stupid.'

'Leave me alone, Godfrey, or let's talk about something else.'

'You don't want to talk about it?'

'I don't really see . . . what there is to talk about.'

Half an hour later, she was lying on the bed. He was sitting in the chair, listening.

★   ★   ★

' . . . I suppose it's what happens to a lot of people. I was drying myself after a bath and I felt this lump, well, it was hardly even a lump, it was so small. Ramsey was there, he was making breakfast, and I went into the kitchen and just said . . . just asked him to look at it. He said it was probably just a gland or something and I should go to the doctor, but I didn't want to, it seemed so stupid. Our doctor's a great friend of Ramsey's, everyone goes to him, his mother, Flora, all his sisters when they're pregnant or the children have measles. I didn't want to . . . get involved in all that, I'd sooner have gone to someone else. It's funny looking back on it now, but we had a kind of quarrel about this—well, an argument. We never really quarrelled. Anyway, in the end he rang up this doctor and I went round to see him. This was a Wednesday morning, it was marvellous weather— May, there was a heat-wave. I was just pleased to put off going to work, I thought I'd walk back through the park and maybe have lunch with Ramsey—what I can't understand now is that I didn't know, I mean I didn't have even the faintest idea that it was . . . already over between Ramsey and me. And yet all the way to the doctor's I was thinking about him as though it was over, and not wanting it to be, and planning stupid things like . . . oh, I don't know, buying him something, or telling him I loved him. I wanted to tell him I'd loved him. I even thought he might get run over during the day, and I wouldn't have told him. Maybe I knew, really, but I don't think so.

'Anyway. The doctor said it was a small cyst,

nothing, but it would have to come out. He left me for a long time while he phoned the surgeon. I looked at his books but I didn't take any out of the shelf in case he thought I was prying ... I didn't want to seem interested at all, although I could have read all about cysts if I'd wanted to. I did want to, but I didn't want him to know. He's a very ... impartial man, very discreet and all that, and I had no idea what he thought about Ramsey and Flora and me. Flora is a very free sort of person. The kind of person who says exactly what she thinks, at least she makes you believe she says exactly what she thinks. I knew she would have talked to him about me for hours, so I didn't want him to know me, I just wanted to keep quiet.

He said I was to see the surgeon at two—I'd thought it would be next week, or the week after. I rang Ramsey, but the line was engaged, and after that I couldn't find a telephone. It's funny how exactly I remember that day, I feel I remember every minute of it. I went into The Times Bookshop in Wigmore Street to buy *The War of Two Worlds* for Michael—he's our landlady's son—and they said they didn't have any call for H. G. Wells, but they might have a gift edition of *The Invisible Man* in leather.

'Anyway, the surgeon looked at me and said it was a small cyst but it had better come out, he could nick it out in a moment or dissolve it, anyway I'd only be in hospital overnight. I still thought it would be weeks before I could get a bed—you know, you're always hearing about it—but when I asked him when it would be he said, Ha, just like that, and clapped his hands, there's no time like the present. So I really

[149]

didn't think. It seemed like having a tooth out. I just went home and got my things for one night, and left a note for Ramsey, and I was in bed at the hospital by six. It wasn't even twelve hours since I'd found the thing. When the surgeon came he sat down on my bed, he seemed rather embarrassed. He said the chances were one in ten thousand that they'd find anything more, but just in case they did he'd like my permission to go ahead . . . I laughed and said he could do anything he liked. When Ramsey came, I was under sedation. I didn't know he was there.

'Well, anyway. When I woke up it was gone. I I knew it was. He didn't have to tell me. Apparently he told me while I was still under the anaesthetic, and it seems I cried. But I don't remember.'

*   *   *

There was a long silence. She had almost forgotten Godfrey. As she began to remember him again she sat up, swung her legs off the bed, smiled at him vaguely.

'Well. That's it. You wanted to know.'

'Yes. Thank you.'

'You're only the second person I've told.'

'You didn't mind . . .'

'Of course not,' she said impatiently.

'What happened to Ramsey?'

'I . . . thought I wanted to live by myself. He went back to Flora. He didn't want to go, but . . . we couldn't have managed.'

'Are you sure?'

[150]

'Yes. At the time. I was quite sure.'

'But now?'

She got up and poured herself a drink, pulled back the curtains and looked out. It was still raining. 'I haven't heard from him.'

'Is MacNeish the other person you told?'

'No.'

'Good. I'm glad.'

She walked across the room, unnecessarily folded a piece of tissue paper, and walked back again. She didn't want to ask him, but she did: 'Why?'

'Because I think he's irresponsible.'

'I don't expect him to be responsible.'

'I know.'

He picked up a belt from the floor and began winding it round his fist. She felt he was at a loss, and that it served him right. He had been trying to help, and now found there was nothing he could do to help. This was the reaction she feared most, people's sense of helplessness.

'What will you do,' he asked, 'when you go back?'

The worst question, since the answer depended on her belief in living. She answered it as honestly as she could: 'I don't know.'

'I'm sure you shouldn't live alone. Haven't you got some girl-friend or something. . . ?'

'Look, Godfrey,' she said gently. 'You aren't responsible either. I wish I hadn't told you.'

'Don't please say that. I just feel so . . . useless.'

'That's what I mean. I don't want to make you feel useless. The best thing you can do for me, if you want

[151]

to do something, is just . . . accept it. I mean, why should you make me feel that I've done something terrible to *you*?'

'You shouldn't feel that, of course.'

'No, but don't you see I do, if you're so upset, if you're so concerned?'

'Would you sooner I didn't give a damn?'

'I think so. Yes.'

'Is that how you're trying to persuade yourself Ramsey feels?'

'I don't know what Ramsey feels.'

'I can make a pretty good guess. He feels bloody.'

'You don't know Ramsey . . .'

'He made you go to the doctor, he reads what you write, that's enough.'

'Is it?'

He got up, unwinding the belt and dropping it on the bed. 'It's a good deal more than most people have. You can't be responsible for other people either, you know. They feel what they feel, and they do what they think they have to do. There's nothing you can do about it.' He put his hand on her shoulder for a moment. 'I know you're going to hate this. I just wish you had something to . . . fall back on.'

'You mean God.'

'I mean something.'

She said, with difficulty, 'I think about dying. It seems . . . a good deal easier than living, if you see what I mean. I'm . . . not afraid of it. If I were, it might be different.'

'But God is a way in, not a way out.'

'I have to find my own way in, Godfrey.'

'Of course. You might write something. That might be a way in.'

'I'm too frightened.'

'Perhaps if you stopped being so brave about death you might have a bit more courage about living. Hell, any fool can die. Wallace Frogmore can die.'

She smiled bleakly. 'I must go to bed, Godfrey. Perhaps I'll see you . . .'

'In London. Yes, I should like that. I'd like you to meet my wife, too. She's a wise woman.'

She felt they were now inaudible to each other. 'Yes, let's do that. I'll ring you when I get back.'

'Please.'

She walked with him to the door, knowing that there was something else he wanted to say and hoping that he wouldn't. He hesitated. She said quickly, 'I'll send you a postcard from the Coast, if I get there.'

'Yes. You're sure you're . . . all right?'

She pretended to misunderstand. 'I'm fine. Very sleepy.'

'No. They said that you're . . . quite all right now?'

'Yes, Godfrey. Sound as a bell.'

He was inching away, puzzled, good and well meaning. When he had gone she was feverish and sick, overwhelmed by a sense of hopelessness she had not felt for many months.

12

IN THE plane the stewardesses wore hats like hearts clamped to the sides of their heads, the Captain urged his passengers to sit back, relax and enjoy the trip; they climbed to twenty-two thousand feet and headed south. Her excitement at the prospect of meeting him came back suddenly, like a name she had forgotten; all night in her sleep she had been worrying what is it? what is it? but it had gone to the edge of her mind and she couldn't remember. The night before a birthday, Christmas Eve? But when she had woken up there had been nothing but the rain, the packing, the memory of Godfrey's pity and sadness making her feel totally discouraged. Now there was very little time, and she had no plan. Supposing I don't tell him at all, just let it happen? No—the whole scene shot behind her eyes, as it is supposed to do when you're drowning—that would be terrible, impossible. Make it as casual, then, as telling him . . . make it casual, throw it away: 'By the way, I had this . . .' Above all, don't let him think it matters. I've got arms, legs, body, all the rest of me, he wants me, what's the difference? Make a joke of it, two for the price of one, do anything. But what? What shall I

do? It will all happen. When it's happened, you'll
know what you did. Not until then. She set up her
mirror and composed a face in the glaring light of
the sky. When she had finished, a man sitting across
the aisle nodded to her and smiled: 'You did a great
job there,' he said. She smiled back, thanking him
for doing her good.

It was only a week since they had arrived at this
airport from England. This time she carried her own
case and hurried up the long ramp, her heart beating
faster and her throat dry. When she got into the
baggage hall she saw him standing behind the plate-
glass screen. He was leaning against a pillar and as he
turned she waved. But it was not him, it was a man
with a beard. She walked towards the doors, trying
to walk slowly in case he had seen her.

'Would Miss Muriel Rowbridge go to the Domestic
Arrivals desk, please. Miss Muriel Rowbridge.'

'Where is the Domestic Arrivals desk?'

'Right over there, ma'am.'

'I was told to come here. Miss Rowbridge.'

'Ah, yes. We have a message for you, Miss
Rowbridge.'

The message said: 'Would you ring Mr. MacNeish,'
and gave the number. In the phone booth she waited
for a few moments, trying to steady her hands and
voice.

'Hullo? Alex?'

'Oh. Muriel. Hi. Did you have a good flight?'

'Yes.'

'I'm sorry I couldn't make it. Things got complicated. Where will you be staying in town?'

'At the . . .'

'Sorry. I didn't catch it.'

'St. George.'

'Well, why don't I call you this evening. We've got to go out to dinner, so it'll be early, about six. O.K.?'

'No,' she lied, 'I won't be there at six.' She swallowed hard, pressing one hand against her mouth to keep the sound in. 'Maybe we could have lunch tomorrow.'

'Sorry, Sundays are out. We could have a drink, though, around twelve. How would that be?'

'All right. Yes, all right.'

'I'll call by, then, around twelve. Take care. Enjoy yourself.'

He found out. Before I went away that night. He knows. She was unable to be reasonable, this seemed the only explanation. She thought of getting a flight, now, back to England, but considered the idea as momentarily as she would have considered suicide. Twenty-three hours to be got through—sitting on the kingsize bed alone? She rang Robert. When he heard her voice he was silent, and she had to ask again, 'Hullo? Robert? Are you there?'

'Yes. Yes, I am here.'

'I'm at the airport. Could you come and fetch me?'

'Of course.'

'I'll be . . . you know, where the seats are.'

'Which car would you prefer?'

She pretended to laugh. 'I don't know. The Bentley.'

'Very well. I'll be with you in half an hour.'

She went and sat on a bench and took out the note-book, leafing slowly through it as though to discover her own history: 'The stewardess is demonstrating the life-jacket. . . . One way of scaring oneself stiff is to imagine looking into a mirror and finding no reflection . . . 250,000 lakes and 140 million acres . . . I don't know that once I'm discovered, dug out and exposed to the ordinary human air, they won't turn away in disgust . . . He sang these few bars like a bus blows its horn round Mediterranean corners . . . I feel like a rib shouting to be plucked out . . . I want to live all over again, exactly as I have done, but in your sight . . . You have to be worth it . . . How can I feel so badly unfaithful to someone who has nothing to do with me? . . . When we first met, he told me that he had been devoured for ten years. His whole idea of loving was omnivorous . . . Terminalia berries, eugenia bark, dandelion and logwood, heart-wood and prickly pear . . . I almost resent you for wasting my time . . . it seemed that the only thing to do was to occupy herself with someone else, it hardly mattered who . . .' That was the end, the last thing to read as she sat waiting for Robert; and what did it all add up to? What was she writing about, and why? A woman in despair; a child in love.

She unclipped the ball-point and wrote quickly: ' "Why do you have to go out on a Saturday, you never see the children, what about us, what about me—inconsiderate, unloving, if you weren't you'd call the airport and leave a message for the woman. Of course you don't *have* to go, you never keep any of your promises to me, why should you keep them

[157]

to other people? Oh, all right, if it's more important what some English woman journalist thinks, everything's more important nowadays than we are . . . I'm *not* crying, it's just that I get so lonely, and after all the children do have a father, it's not that they haven't *got* a father . . ."

'No, that's probably too obvious. Anyway, she's perfectly right. Robert comes crawling in the Bentley. I don't have to tell him anything, I don't have to make anything up.

'And you're saying all the time I love you, I love you, everything stupid I shall do during the next few days is because I love you. You are the only person I would go to at any time, regardless of anything. The only person I want to be with. Why couldn't I say it?

'Feelings, by themselves, have no words. So there are no words, and when you try to force feelings into words it is hopeless. I write like a sixteen-year-old. What do I want? To feel this sentimental sacrament, this ceremony being perpetually performed, over and over, in what I call my heart? Is that all? To fantasise, to day-dream, to dream. It's all I can expect, having nothing to offer. Nothing but trouble. But it's certainly not enough.

'It was bad to ask for lunch tomorrow. Bad to let out the faintest sound of harried hurry (but the time's so short, don't you understand?). Too much complication spoils everything, however almost invisible, imperceptible, that everything may be. Things should always seem simple, even when they're not. So I lecture myself, and can't smile.'

She looked up and saw Robert coming towards

her across the hall. He did not kiss her, for which she was grateful, but stood looking at her for a moment before picking up her suitcase. Then he said, 'You're here,' and took her arm, almost running her out of the airport. The small crowd round the Bentley moved reluctantly away.

'You know, while you were away a friend lent me his new Honda-450, it runs at about 7500 to 8000 revs, quite a machine, the fourth gear clicks in between sixty and seventy. It was terribly cold here—was it cold with you?—but he gave me a black oilcloth suit and a helmet and I went on the track and hit a ton. Actually I only confessed to 80 mph, not to worry him. And do you know I couldn't be frightened. I tried again next morning, same thing. Concentration, concern, care—but no fear. I don't know what to make of it. I'd imagined that past seventy I would be shaking. You still think I drive too slowly?'

'No, of course not. Why did you want to be frightened?'

'I was bored.' He hesitated. 'I missed you.'

She didn't say anything, too sad to find any irony in the situation.

'Did you get my letters? I just wanted to write you something, I hope the Doestoevsky didn't offend you ...' He prattled on, excited as a child. She had remembered his silence; he had frequently told her to be quiet. What had she talked about, what kind of a person had she been? She couldn't remember; last weekend seemed like her childhood.

He pulled up in a side street. 'I have to get some drink—I didn't drink all the time you were away, you know that? I'm not meant to park here, would you mind staying in the car?'

'Of course not.'

'Thank you.' He kissed her hand, exuberant, and ran off across the street. She was cheating him, and he had no idea. He thought she had come back to be with him.

Two boys of about twelve years old had stopped on the pavement and were admiring the Bentley. They wore sneakers and striped T-shirts and baggy jeans, their cropped heads glinting like sandpaper. They walked slowly up and down from stem to stern of the amazing vehicle, remarking on the great pop-eyed headlamps, the bumpers, the running boards. One of them, braver than the other, came up to her; she wound the window down.

'Excuse me, miss—how old is it, the car?'

'I don't know exactly. I should think it's about 1938, wouldn't you?' As old as herself. He whistled slowly. 'Gee, that's pretty old. Where you from?'

'England.'

'That's an English car, a Bentley, huh?'

'Would you like to get in?'

'Sure would.'

She got out and let him sit in her seat. He touched the mahogany dashboard, peered at the dials, tested the gear lever, stretched out and put his feet on the clutch and accelerator. He wanted to know if the speaking tube worked, so the friend came and sat in the back and blew down it.

'Don't do that. Say something.'

'What'll I say?'

[160]

'Oh boy . . .' He shook his head in parental despair. 'You put flowers in this? Real ones?'

'Of course, if you want to.'

'That's certainly some car.' He got out, held the door for her while she got in, closed it gently. He and the friend walked round it once more, then he came up and said to her, 'My friend says it's bullet-proof.' He lowered his voice and added confidentially, 'I don't believe him.'

'I'm sure it may be.'

'No,' he said. 'No. It's not bullet-proof.'

She smiled at him, shrugging her shoulders as though to say well, we all have to take risks. They wandered off with backward glances, still arguing.

*   *   *

That night, in the severe loneliness that comes after loveless sex (the loneliness of sexless love is bleak, but bearable), she tried to ring Ramsey in London. She knew that there would be no comfort in it, but even the idea of being included, in the shape of a white telephone receiver, in their bed, made her feel less desolate. She knew it would be five o'clock in the morning in London, and she thought quite clearly that once they had been woken they probably wouldn't go to sleep again for some time. It seemed the most foolish thing, apart from ringing MacNeish, that she could think of doing.

'. . . Hullo?' It was Flora. He hated answering the telephone in case it made some demand on him.

'It's Muriel . . .'

[161]

'Muriel! My God, you're not back, are you?'

'No. I'm sorry to wake you up. Is Ramsey there?'

'Hang on a minute.' She was struggling out of the bedclothes, turning on the light perhaps; shaking his shoulder. 'No, love, he's not here. He hasn't been here all week. He went back to the flat on Sunday.'

'You mean . . . my flat?'

'If you like. He doesn't want you to know, though. Lady C. said you wouldn't be back till Monday at the earliest and you might be going to some coast or other, is that right? Anyway, he thinks he's imposing on you or something.'

'But I'm not there, how could he . . . ?'

'That's what he means. He swore he'd get somewhere by this weekend, but . . . well, you know Ramsey.'

'But . . . why isn't he with you?'

'It didn't work out, love. I suppose I'm too used to my independence. Anyway, that's where you'll find him. Are you all right? Having a good time? No, you can't be having a good time if you want to talk to Ramsey. But are you all right, darling?'

'Yes. I'm fine. Thank you, then. I'm sorry I woke you . . .'

'Take care of yourself. See you soon.'

In the other room Robert was asleep, naked, face down across the single bed. The light was still on, the floor littered with clothes, empty glasses, spilt ashtrays. She wished she could wake him up and talk to him, but he didn't care to be talked to, he seemed to want to protect himself against being told anything. She couldn't ring Ramsey if he didn't want her to know that he was at the flat. She knew that nothing she could say would make him feel less guilty and discovered. He was hiding there, and she must allow him a place to hide. There was no one in the entire world to talk to, she must seal herself up and live in herself like a hermit.

Cupping her hands under Robert's body, she moved him in his sleep to the side of the bed and lay down beside him, stretching back to turn off the light. He moaned, and flung himself towards her, holding her tightly.

*   *   *

'Sunday 12.25 St. George's Hotel, shaking, shaken out of shape, in a bad way, falling on this meeting like someone who hasn't eaten, who hasn't breathed for days. Bad, bad. How to disguise, integrate again; how to leave again, how to go back to the person who suffocates and traps me. That's so unfair, oh think of that later.

'Behave well, to behave well is to be well, the only way to be happy. If he doesn't want to know that he's food and air, don't tell him. I think I must go back to England, I think I must write and write and write and not stop for a year, I think it's time to remember and stop inventing. I drew ALEX on the marble table with my finger, the writing let off a little steam. There have been times in the huis clos of the last twenty-four hours when I've felt demented. It's 12.30 exactly. Don't meet 1.30 before it happens . . .'

*   *   *

[163]

'Shall we go to the bar?'

'If you like.' She had hoped that they would go somewhere else, but, of course, his time was short. The bar was very full; they groped to a small table and sat on small gilt chairs; he ordered two martinis.

'So what have you been doing with yourself since you got back?' He didn't wait for an answer. 'I'm sorry about yesterday, but all hell had broken loose when I got back from St. Andrews. Joss had heard I was still seeing Evie, so she'd been round to see her, both of them were on to me the minute I got back. I tell you, it's been rough. Naturally, when she heard I was going to the airport to meet you yesterday she blew her top—Saturday, the kids, me never seeing the kids—which is a bloody lie, I see them more than she does—everybody else being more important than they are, the usual spiel. I can tell you, Muriel, I'm worn out. I mean, hell, I've got work to do. I'd just like to say the hell with the lot of them and go off somewhere.'

'Well . . . you're going to the Coast, aren't you?'

'Only for a couple of days. So what's up with you? When do you go back to London?'

'I . . . don't know exactly.'

'I may be coming over in the spring. We must meet.'

'Yes. Yes, we must.'

'I imagine you have a pretty swinging time in London, don't you?' He smiled at her, touching her hair for a moment with the back of his hand. 'You want another?'

'Thank you.' If she had another she might suddenly

break open, divert and dazzle him with tricks of some sort. 'I can't bear this much longer,' she said.

'Can't bear what?'

'Sitting here being so polite to each other.'

He withdrew very slightly. 'Are we being polite? I hadn't noticed. Would you sooner we insulted each other?'

'I wouldn't know how. What would you find insulting?'

He looked at her, it seemed, for the first time, then made his pronouncement: 'You're a funny girl, Muriel. I don't understand you.'

She smiled with all the power of her eyes. 'So if you don't understand me—I'm funny?'

'Clever women make me uncomfortable. I never know what's going to happen next. Joss effects me like that, after all these years. She makes me itch.'

'Or gives you a stomach-ache?'

'That's right. I get the most terrible stomach-aches. Now with Evie I feel perfectly well. How do you explain that?'

'And how do you feel with me?'

'Well . . .' He scratched the back of his neck, grinning. 'A bit itchy. I don't know what you're driving at.'

'Don't you?' She was trembling, certain that he must feel it. 'You do, really.'

He picked up his glass, but didn't drink, peering down into it. After a long pause he said, 'It's a bad time, Muriel. I told you. I can't stand complications.'

Which is why, she wanted to say, you have so many of them. She said nothing, waiting for him, leaving the rim of her glass between her lips, not drinking.

'Joss has been very upset. She thought it was all over, you see. I've hurt her a great deal. Well, I've hurt both of them . . . You see what I mean?'

'It can't just be a choice between Joss and Evie for ever.' She drank quickly. 'You never will choose, anyway.'

'That's what bugs me, don't you see? The world's packed with women, and for every one of them there's a balls-up. God, what a prospect!' He took her hand, unclenching it, feeling the fingers. 'Still tense. I like you very much, you know. Well—you knew that at the party, didn't you?'

'I hoped so,' she said dryly.

'We'll see each other in London—promise?'

She blurted it out long before she was ready to say it: 'Shall I come to the Coast?'

'No.' Her wrist was circled with his finger and thumb; he pressed it gently. 'Now I've hurt you.'

'No.'

'But you're hurt. I can tell.'

She smiled. There was a tremendous relief, as well as what felt like an agonising sadness. 'I hurt myself. So do Joss and Evie, actually. We've all got do-it-yourself hurt kits. People like you just take the credit.'

'But you're angry.'

'I'm not.' She said it for the first and last time, but in the voice she might use to a child: 'I love you.'

'Well . . . I'm sorry. We'll make up for it in London. Here, you'd better give me your phone number . . .'

He wrote it down on the back of an envelope, stuffed it into his pocket. She got up. From now on, what she was doing seemed impossible, as though she were handcuffed to him and yet, miraculously, able to walk away.

'You'll be late for lunch.'

'God, yes. That would be the end.' He flung down some money on the table and took her arm. 'Are you going out? Can I give you a lift somewhere?'

'No, thanks.' In the lobby she said, 'Well. Goodbye. I hope it all gets sorted out.'

'So do I. I can't stand much more of it, I can tell you.' He kissed her on the mouth. 'I'm sorry about it all.'

'There's nothing to be sorry about. Call me when you get to London.'

'I will. Goodbye for now. Take care.'

She turned and walked towards the bookstall. He had gone. She hurried to the Ladies', locked herself in and sat there doubled up, silent, unconsciously rocking herself with grief.

*   *   *

'Muriel? Is that you?'

She didn't answer. He had given her a key, he had been sitting waiting for her, reading the Sunday papers, he had not asked her where she was going. She dropped her handbag and pulled off her jacket, looked up the number of the airline, dialled the number.

'Hullo? I want to make a reservation for London—tonight, if possible.' Waiting, she turned to look at him. The papers had fallen on the floor. He was sitting with his elbows on his knees, his fists clenched against his forehead.

He looked up at her. 'You have to go?'

'Yes . . . Twenty-forty-five? No, economy. What's the flight number? I see. Yes. Thank you, I'll be there.' She put down the receiver. 'I have to, Robert.'

'Could I ask why?'

'Because . . . Because it's my nature.'

He came and held her closely. She began to cry. He held her until the crying lessened, then put her down on the sofa and brought her a drink.

She shook her head. 'I don't want it.'

'Then don't have it. Tell me really why you have to go.'

'I can't . . . I don't know. I have to go anyway, so . . .'

'But you haven't heard from England? They haven't asked you to go back?'

She shook her head again.

'Then I tell you what. I'm free tomorrow and Tuesday. I can be free. Why don't we have lunch, drive out to the country, spend the night in a motel somewhere. Tomorrow we'll go and take the boat in, and tomorrow night, if you like, we can stay in my house.'

'Your house?'

'It's got four walls and a roof. You might not be comfortable there . . .'

'I'm sure I would. But it's no use, Robert . . .' She

[168]

began to cry again, sick with herself. 'It's no . . .
bloody use.'

'What isn't?'

'Me. You. Anything.'

'That doesn't matter,' he said, practical. 'I want you
to come with me. I want it more . . . than I have
wanted anything in a very long time.'

She looked at him carefully: the wide gaze, almost
a stare, the neat face disrupted by a trembling mouth.
He did want her to go. He had been thinking about
it the whole week. She had promised him that she
would go. She had asked him to tell her something,
some story. Ramsey was in the flat and she couldn't
go back without telling him—was that a reason?
Robert slid his hand under her shirt, held it against
her left breast. He was imploring her. The real reason
was that it didn't matter whether she stayed or went.
Quite clearly, nothing mattered.

She smiled uncertainly. 'All right. I don't suppose
it matters.'

'Thank you. Could I ask you one more thing?'

'What is it?'

His hand moved across to the hard, cold artificial
breast. She couldn't feel it. 'Don't wear this thing.
It's not necessary.'

'All right. If you like. It doesn't matter.'

He jumped to his feet, pulling her after him, a dead
weight. 'Then quickly. Let's get ready. Yes? Let's go!'
He became a whirlwind in which she moved slug-
gishly. She heard him telephoning the airline, post-
poning her reservation until Tuesday. She took off
her brassière and threw it into a suitcase, pulling on a

[169]

sweater over her bare skin. He gave her a leather jacket, saying peremptorily, 'Wear this. You'll be cold.' At the last moment, just as they were going out of the front door, she ran back and got the brassière, pushing it deep into the pocket of his coat.

13

HE TOOK the Ferrari. Since nothing mattered any more, she wrote MacNeish a postcard—it showed the grill room of St. George's Hotel in heavy colour—saying that she was leaving on Tuesday and asking him to take her to the airport. She gave him Robert's telephone number and asked him to call her on Tuesday evening. The uselessness of this seemed entirely suitable to her. Not to try and see him again, not to write the postcard, would have been to assume that there was a clear future in which she must try to behave sensibly, and survive. She asked Robert to stop at a post office, got a stamp out of the machine and posted the card to MacNeish's office.

They drove. She nursed her sadness and resignation and sense of being in love. Every time Robert spoke, or sang one of his warning snatches, it was like a drill on a raw nerve. She felt like a whore, but thought that possibly whores behaved better, since there was no need for them to deceive anyone and it was doubtful whether they suffered much from love.

'I'm sorry,' she said. 'I'll come out of it soon. I feel as though I've hit between the eyes or below the belt or something.'

He nodded, as though he understood. After this he stopped talking and singing.

*   *   *

The sweater was warm and slightly abrasive against her skin. She felt very free without the armour, able to move naturally inside her clothes. After a while, a simple question began to interest her: why, if you have one breast, is it necessary to pretend to have two? A leg or arm, yes; they are necessary for walking or holding. The only function of breasts is to feed children, and an artificial breast will not feed a child anyway. You can walk with an artificial leg, or carry with an artificial arm, but an artificial breast is useless except to assuage vanity and make other people comfortable.

She asked him, 'Why did you want me to take it off?'

He thought for a moment. 'Because I prefer you as you are.'

She considered this for a long time. Somewhere far below the indifference and sadness a small flicker of excitement leapt up. She waited, alert, for it to go out, but it grew, running and spreading. 'Because I prefer you as you are.' There was something tremendously important in this statement. She did not know yet why it was so important. She leant forward in the car, clasping her hands together.

The sensation was unknown to her, she could not recognise it. It had the appearance of a bird breaking slowly out of its shell, a chrysalis crumbling, a snake moving deliberately but thoughtlessly out of its skin.

[172]

Like the bird, the butterfly, the snake, she did not know what was happening to her. She was growing. She was materialising, becoming re-embodied. She was visible. She could be seen.

None of this was articulate; but it was immensely clear, exact and accurate. When you aren't seen, hidden within a protective shell, you live always in secret, alone, the world's eyes give back no reflection. You have only your own knowledge of your existence to keep you alive, and even that may be illusory. The sense of liberation came with this plain corroboration of her being: 'I prefer you as you are.'

She looked at him. He was driving steadily, his face expressionless. She wanted to say something, but she was like someone struggling with a vision, the revelation was becoming too bright and immense to be put into words.

She said, 'Something's happened.'

'Yes. I know. I felt it.'

'I'm . . . going to write something.'

Without turning, he took her hand, smiled, released her hand, but said nothing.

She had found, after all this time of searching, an image: myself as I am, I prefer myself as I am. The implications came crowding in on her with the impact of light, air and sound after a long imprisonment. Boldness and freedom were both available. She could do anything she wanted to do.

But what should she write? That ought to be a frightening, dampening question; it always had been before. Once upon a time there was a frog and a scorpion, and in the end the scorpion said, 'I prefer

[173]

myself as I am': the story of fear and blindness, love and illusion, trust and self-realisation. The story of the handle being too near the lintel, the place the path reached when it had crossed the field, the story of not being seen and not being believed. She would write it having one breast, in the knowledge that she might die. The exhilaration was almost more than she could bear. Pulses were beating all over her body, she was breaking out in fires. The idea that she could be who she was, feel and think and function in her own right, without artificiality, was magnificent. She wanted the whole sky to break open with a great shout, a thousand trees to burst into flames, the road to become a ceremonial way. As for Robert, her gratitude to him was a form of love she had never felt before, it was as strong and all-inclusive as a prayer on being raised from the dead. She wanted to give him something—more than something, a heap, a caravan, a procession of gifts, she wanted to load him with her own happiness. Nothing could alter this feeling; it was firmly based and sprung from a positive reality. She held it in, but it shone through her eyes, filled her whole body with pleasure.

They stopped to board a ferry going across a lake. She climbed out of the car and ran to the gift shop on the side of the road. She searched impatiently through paperweights and snowstorms, engraved wallets, key-rings and table-mats. He was inching the car to the head of the queue. She bought a complicated pocket knife and a white nautical cap with gold braid and ran back to the car as he was driving it on to the ferry. She gave him the knife.

'For you. It has things for everything. Things for performing abortions on beavers. You mustn't lose it.'

'Well, you must wear the cap.'

The lake was squally, gusts of rain and spray blown against the windscreen. A man in a big sedan alongside them wound down his window and shouted something. When her window was down the rain hit her full in the face.

'That's a very fine car you've got there.'

'Thank you,' she said, as though it were her own.

'You folks from England?'

'I am.'

'I was there once. Halifax. You know Halifax?' Her happiness reached him through the rain. Honeymooners, he thought, and because he was that kind of man, added: God bless 'em. 'Well, I suppose it's quite a ways from London. What's the car, then?'

Robert leant across her and explained about the car. She wanted to hold him, but it wasn't necessary. Her enchantment held both of them, he was electrified merely by touching her.

They reached the other side. 'Well,' the man said, 'have a good time, whatever your endeavour may be.' It was a benediction.

She said, 'I've never been so happy in my life.'

'Never?'

'I think never. When will you tell me?'

'Tonight.'

'I want to buy you a drink now. Champagne.'

'You can't drink champagne here, but I'll take a martini.'

They smiled at each other, as though they were conspirators. He drove into the neon-lit parking lot of a roadside bar called Aladdin's Cave—treasure piled to the roof, the magical lamp in her hands. She felt the brassière in her pocket and in her elation she thought she would bury it somewhere, have a ceremonial fire. She had never felt more confident, swaggering into the bar in his jacket, loaded with gold and power; when she was inside she took the jacket off, he smiled now with a kind of pain and said, 'You look wonderful.'

'You needn't say that any more.'

'I do need to say it. I need to say many things. Impossible.'

'Then let's just be here.'

The bar was a dark horseshoe, only two women in hats sitting in the gloom. One wall was glass, and through this there was a kind of garage or storehouse which had been painted entirely mauve. There were mauve lights, mauve tablecloths on mauve tables, a mauve grand piano at which sat an enormous wrestler in a mauve vest pounding the keys with his great fists. The mauve electric-light bulbs on the wall wrote his name: Billy Bunn. The mauve electric sign on the glass window announced: Fascination Room. Billy Bunn assaulted 'Deep Purple'; his arpeggios were a load of bricks falling downstairs, his chords had the fine panache of a sledgehammer on the keys. When he finished they applauded warmly, he gave them a wrestler's handshake through the window and crashed vigorously into 'September Song' . . .

> 'For it's a long, long time
> From May to November,
> And the days grow short
> When you reach September . . .
> And the autumn weather
> Turns the leaves to flame,
> And I haven't got time
> For the waiting game . . .'

Difficult feelings, expressed with such facility that even Billy Bunn could get the idea, rolling his great body about on the small mauve stool.

> 'But the days whittle down
> To a precious few,
> September . . . November . . .
> And these few precious days
> I'll spend with you,
> These precious days
> I'll spend with you . . .'

She couldn't stop smiling, now and then holding her hands to her face as though catching an over-flowing glee. It was not necessary or possible to explain to him. Every sensation, the sweater moving against her skin, the thick glass in her hand, the pantomime light and sound, was acute, in focus for the first time. They talked only about the place itself, as though nothing else had ever existed: they speculated about the mauve, about Billy Bunn's piano lessons, about his relationship with the barmaid, about the sexual nature of the two women in hats. An hour, an hour and a half, went by; she wanted to be encapsulated, sleeping beautified there for ever, but Robert said they must go and find a motel.

It was on the shore of the lake, the black water lapping and sucking at an old landing stage, the shapes of what seemed paper boats bobbing in the darkness. The cabin had a wrought-iron screen over the frosted-glass front door. When they let themselves in she threw her arms high in the air and said, 'It's Paradise,' not meaning that it was delightful or comfortable or pleasant, but that it was in fact a state and place of happiness which she had never experienced before, a state in which prayer and joy became the same thing, an inexpressible gratitude for the pine walls, the bed with candlewick cover, the vast television set, the paper cups sealed up for hygiene. He caught her hand and pulled her down on to the bed.

'You're possessed,' he said.

'Yes.'

'Do you want to make love?'

'Yes.'

She took off her clothes and leant, half kneeling, against the end of the bed, waiting for him. He lay on the bed and looked at her for some minutes. It was so quiet that they could hear the lake moving outside.

14

'ROBERT'S story:

'10 a.m. Robert was walking across the lawn with Arthur Massingham after borrowing a weed spray, and spoke briefly with Brian Stevens.

'10.10. Brian met Jim Eysen who was going to paint his boat and they arranged a tennis game for 11 o'clock.

'10.15. At the shore, Robert, who was 200 yards out in his rowing boat in calm waters, talked with Brian. The skies were sunny and a light breeze was blowing with enough force to cause them to raise their voices over the intervening distance.

'10.15. Reg and Julie Hemmings came down to the shore to rig their boat, prior to going sailing.

'10.30. Whilst reading further along the beach, Brian watched Robert and Eleanor put out in their sailboat under the jibsail and then hoist the mainsail before sailing on a reach toward Seal Island. The water was quite calm and a light breeze was blowing. The sun was shining.

'10.50. The wind was freshening and the waves were beginning to rise. Brian mentioned to Reg and

Julie his concern about Robert and Eleanor, who were by this time about a mile from shore and appearing to have trouble going about. (Robert explained later that at this point Eleanor was at the tiller and he was showing her the technique of 'coming about'. It is apparent that they were in the partial leas of Seal Island and unaware of the changing conditions.)

'11.10 a.m. The wind had risen strongly and heavy waves were forming. Brian discussed with Jim Eysen and Phil Rawlings (both of whom had served in the Navy) his concern for Robert and Eleanor, although their sails were still visible.

'11.15 a.m. From the lawn of the house, which is elevated about 30 feet above the water, Brian saw no sign of the sails and immediately called Phil and Jim. The boat was not visible and they discussed the possibility of it having put into Seal to wait out the squall that had arisen.

'11.20 a.m. It was thought that something should be done and Phil and Brian asked Reg for his sailboat, in order to go out after Robert and Eleanor. Reg agreed and went up to his house to get the sails, but by this time Phil believed, rightly, that because of the intensity of the wind and the rapidly rising waves, it would be impossible to sail.

'11.25 a.m. Phil and Brian set off for Camp Lodge, a mile from the harbour, to borrow a power boat. Arthur and Jim went up the inland creek to borrow the motor boat of a fisherman who had recently come in.

'11.35 a.m. Phil and Brian arrived at Camp Lodge,

where no power boat was yet prepared for the water. Mr. Brenner, the owner, who is a resident and knows the lake well, searched with binoculars and the capsized boat was spotted in the water between, and this side of Blair and Seal Islands, about $1\frac{1}{2}$ to $1\frac{3}{4}$ miles away.

'11.50 a.m. Phil and Brian then drove down the coast road looking for a boat, but they were all too light to be launched.

'11.55–12.00. At Mike Martin's camp there was a 14-foot fibreglass power boat with an outboard motor. Some delays ensued because Mr. Martin doubted that the boat could be launched or handled in the now heavy waves pounding the shore, and because his wife and neighbours vociferously opposed the idea.

'However, he agreed to go and it took six men to launch the boat, which after shipping water got under way with Mr. Martin, Phil and Brian.

'11.30 a.m. Jim and Arthur had found a fisherman who assured them that his light, open boat could not get out in the waves, and they recognised it to be true. The fisherman suggested that they go to see a relative who might have a larger boat. Jim and the fisherman went off together and visited several camps but the boats were light and incapable of putting out. Then Jim saw Mr. Martin's power boat with Phil and Brian out in the bay, so he returned to the harbour and called the coastguard at 12.20 exactly.

'11.40 a.m. Meanwhile Arthur had taken a car and headed to the boat yard on the causeway, where on the previous day he had seen two larger power boats. From this direction he would have approached the point of capsize with the waves at his back, giving him a better chance of reaching the area.

'12 noon. The boatyard owner refused to hire a boat under any circumstances, being sure that they could not survive the conditions. He passed Arthur to two men whose newly built houseboat had a 100 h.p. engine and they promptly agreed to try. They left the shore at approximately 12.10.

'12.10 p.m. Mr. Martin in the power boat had to take the waves head-on—any attempts to move off them caused yawing and loss of control—and crossed into the lea of Blair Island, then south, and out again into rough water and the area where Robert and Eleanor had capsized. The conditions, with heavy spray and occasional waves breaking over the boat, forced a narrow course. The search party anticipated that Robert and Eleanor would drift in the N.E. direction of the waves (which was in the direction of Camp Lodge). It was later found that the wind had swung to the west and they had been carried in towards the harbour. The watchers on the lawn being elevated above the water could see through binoculars the capsized boat, with Eleanor and Robert in red life-jackets lying across it from opposite sides, and they could see the power boat about half a mile further out. During the period since capsizing Robert and Eleanor had drifted about three-quarters of a mile. The search was intense but fruitless, and the gasoline supply diminishing. Mr. Martin turned for home with the prayer that they were sheltered by the

[182]

island. The power boat was pulled ashore still in high waves about 12.55 p.m.

'12.30 p.m. Stuart Fletcher and Pete Grossier had returned from a walk at about 12.15 to 12.30 and found the group of people on the lawn watching the overturned sailboat in the distance, perhaps three-quarters of a mile away in rough water. Stuart and Pete set off to seek a boat strong enough to negotiate the conditions of the lake. The waves were very high with the white caps being whipped into spray by the strong and gusting wind. They met Phil and Brian returning, and after discussion they all returned to the harbour.

'12.10–12.15 p.m. Aboard the houseboat, Arthur was on the roof of the cabin with binoculars, directing it to the area between Seal and Blair Islands, closer to the eastern shore than the power boat, which he had seen for a brief period. He estimated that they were in the area at about 12.35 and on the assumption that the wind and waves carried Robert and Eleanor towards Mr. Martin's Camp Lodge, he searched the area. Then the boat ran into terrific waves, such as Arthur had not seen in six years on the lake, and the boat began taking on water, causing the owner to fear that the engine would be swamped. Arthur pressed him to head towards the shore at an angle to the waves, but the owner maintained that the boat would capsize unless they stayed head on to the waves, and thus they headed back. With waves breaking over the bow and heavy spray over the roof, they headed towards the boatyard. Arthur continued to search the area through binoculars, but no to avail, and having seen Mr. Martin's power boat he hoped that a rescue had been made. On the way back they encountered a small coastguard motor boat to whom they described their search and suggested the possibility of searching further inshore. The boats were unable to get close and Arthur could not transfer to the coastguard boat. He returned to harbour between 2.15 and 2.30 p.m.

'12.30 p.m. At the Coast Guard office, Chief Kramer received Jim's call at 12.20 and identified the location on his chart as being between Blair and Seal Islands. The larger coast guard boat was at Wellington which is 2½ hours sailing time away, so he and a colleague headed by car for the causeway and took out their smaller boat at about 12.45 p.m.

'He put the boat out and on the way met Arthur returning in the houseboat. Kramer continued, and searched through binoculars, but the waves again began to fill the boat and he was forced to return. Arriving at the marina after 2 p.m. he got news from the police radio that Eleanor and Robert had been reached and the search had ended. He estimated that the waves were higher than 4 feet and that the winds were in the region of 40–50 miles an hour. He noted that Seal Island was about 2 miles from the harbour and Blair a little further.

'1.15 p.m. Returning to the harbour, Pete, Jim, Stuart, Phil and Brian joined the others and their wives on the lawn. Robert and Eleanor were clearly visible half sitting, half lying across the boat which by this time was on its side. Robert was standing on the mast and Eleanor was crouching on the centre board, her arm being held by Robert. At this point they were half to three-quarters of a mile from shore, the wind had reduced slightly and the waves, though still heavy, no longer had white tops. John Street and Reg ran back up the inland creek and insisted on borrowing the small aluminium power boat from the fisherman. Brian and Stuart ran across to Robert's cabin and launched his little rowing shell. In the urgency of the moment Brian did not stop to put on a life-jacket. The shell, which is canvas and wood, could not have stayed afloat in the white-capped waves earlier; there was now a chance that it could. The same was true for the aluminium power boat. The circumstances made it necessary to take that chance.

'1.20 p.m. Because of the small size of the shell, Brian rowed out alone in the direction of Robert and Eleanor, who were clearly visible to him on the capsized boat. John, who is a retired naval officer, saw that it would be impossible to take his light aluminium power boat across the waves and so moved parallel with the shore and then straight out towards Robert and Eleanor.

'1.30 p.m. Mr. Martin, having news that Robert and Eleanor had not been rescued, came down to the harbour with his son. There he saw through his binoculars that Robert and Eleanor were on opposite sides of the boat and she was crouching on the centre board. They were now about a mile off shore and their life-jackets appeared to be firmly in place. They then drove back to Camp Lodge and loaded on to a tractor a large rowboat of the type used for carrying provisions, and brought it back to the harbour. Arriving at about 1.40 they proceeded to launch the boat.

'1.35 p.m. During the first ten minutes of rowing out towards Robert and Eleanor, Brian had been able, when cresting the waves, to guide himself by their figures across the boat, and then saw that they were no longer on it. It took about ten more minutes to reach them, by which time they were some 40 feet from their boat, Robert behind Eleanor trying desperately but hopelessly to hold her head above the waves. She was blue and her eyes had moved up into her head. Brian pulled her aboard the shell and tried to apply artificial respiration but the shell capsized and Robert again grasped her hair in an attempt to hold her head up.

'By this time John and Reg were on the scene in their light aluminium power boat. Robert continued to hold Eleanor and Brian held Robert, who was cold, and incapable of speaking or understanding. John and Reg got a rope to Brian who wrapped it round his wrist and, holding Robert and Eleanor, was towed by the boat towards the shore. Without a life-jacket, Brian was towed under water, got into difficulties and lost the rope. He told Robert that Eleanor was dead and that he must try to save himself by swimming towards the shore, but Robert was committed and could not leave her.

'Clothed and without a life-jacket Brian was now in difficulties and John and Reg towed him to the shore where others helped him out. John and Reg returned immediately to Robert and got a rope to him, he grasped it but could not hold it. By this time Mr.

Martin and his son Spencer reached the area and pulled Robert and Eleanor aboard their boat. During his years at sea John had seen many fatalities and was convinced, with Brian, that Eleanor was dead in the water.

'2 p.m. Police record a call from Julie who, after seeing Robert and Eleanor in the water, went to phone for an ambulance, emergency equipment, etc. The police reached the harbour at 2.35 p.m.

'Medical opinion supports the belief that Eleanor's death was due to exposure. Her legs and lower body were partially in the water, which was intensely cold (estimated at 38–40 degrees). There were no signs of pain or anguish of any kind. The doctor explained that these conditions cause the slowing of the metabolism of the body, causing drowsiness and numbness, a reduction of perception and no awareness of pain or fear.

*   *   *

'Robert says that they had packed a lunch and were going to sail over to Blair Island for a picnic. They took Eleanor's dog with them, a Yorkshire terrier called Spike. When they were the best part of the way across the winds began to freshen and the waves to rise—for some time they had been in the partial lea of Seal Island and didn't realise how much the wind was rising.

'Nevertheless, Robert thought that a summer squall might be coming and he decided to put into the island as soon as possible. They were very happy. They were sailing well on a starboard reach when, with extraordinary suddenness, heavy winds and high seas hit them simultaneously. The boat was thrown over and upside down. Eleanor was cheerful and swimming a few feet from the boat. They called out to each other, shouting, 'Are you all right?' then Robert told her to climb on to the boat while he grabbed Spike and ducked underneath. There was air under the boat when he put Spike on the upturned thwart and released the life-preservers. Then, swimming from under the boat, he gave Spike to Eleanor and pulled himself up. The waves were heavy but the boat remained relatively stable and Robert fixed and adjusted the life-preserver on Eleanor's chest and back and tied it securely, then fixed his own. For a period of time they were cheerful, certain that they would have seen from the shore and somebody would come for them.

'The weather worsened and the waves grew, the boat was pitched at least twice causing them both to fall into the water. They climbed back each time and by now were being splashed continuously and were feeling the cold. To keep her occupied, Robert got Eleanor to shout with him, and to keep her circulation active he encouraged her to move around as much as possible. He noticed that they were drifting rapidly towards Camp Lodge and in spite of the high waves and the difficult conditions he still thought they would be all right. They did not see either of the boats that came out looking for them.

'By this time the boat had changed its position and

was lying on its side. Eleanor was crouched on the centre board, resting her arms on the side of the upturned boat. Robert was hanging on to the other side of the boat with one hand holding Eleanor's arm. She was watching and warning him of the waves that were coming at his back and he was watching the shore and telling her of the activity he could see on the lawn and the people moving about. They knew they had been sighted.

'The clarity of Robert's recollections diminishes in relation to the time that elapsed, but he remembers seeing the orange-coloured shirt that Brian was wearing coming out to them, he told Eleanor but noticed that there was very little reaction, she appeared to be falling asleep, her eyelids fluttered and her eyes went up. At this stage Robert was standing on the mast, which was horizontal under the water, and leaning over the boat to hold Eleanor, with the dog, which was still alive, between his chest and the boat. While he was encouraging Eleanor to move, he noticed that her feet had trailed off into the water, and then she simply slid away from the boat. For a moment he hoped that she was moving round the boat to his side, but then saw that she was completely still in the water, making no movement of her body or face. He left the dog and slid off the boat towards her, grasping her hair to hold her head above water. It was a few minutes later that Brian arrived in the shell.

*   *   *

[189]

'2 p.m. The people on shore had brought a car down to the beach, had prepared hot drinks, warm blankets, hot-water bottles and hot baths. Within a minute Robert and Eleanor were rushed up to the house. She was immobile and he was cramped, incapable of moving or speaking, and in the view of some observers he was near death. Robert was dumped into a hot bath by Brian, who started to pummel, rub and massage him.

'It had taken about one minute to get them from the shore into the house and Eleanor was immediately taken into the warm living-room where a team of five people worked unceasingly for nearly two hours. Of this group, one was trained in survival technique, including mouth-to-mouth resuscitation. One girl was a physiotherapist and another had had training as a nurse. There was no pulse. A small amount of water was evacuated from Eleanor's lungs and trachea, then mouth-to-mouth artificial respiration was started. This went on until a team equipped with oxygen pumps arrived in response to Julie's call to the police department. The oxygen equipment was not as effective as the previous methods, and artificial respiration was then continued for an hour. No trace of a pulse or heart-beat was achieved at any time and Eleanor had given no indication of response. When Dr. Laslo arrived he continued this treatment for 15 minutes, but after final examination with his stethoscope and a check of Eleanor's eyes, he acknowledged that it was hopeless. The doctor later told Pete Grossier that he believed Eleanor had been dead before being brought out of the water. That Robert was in such a state of exhaustion and was suffering from exposure and shock when rescued, indicates that Eleanor had died some time before and probably at the time when she slipped away from the boat. The time of death was officially recorded as 1.30.'

15

IN THE morning she got up before he was awake and
went down to the lake. It was cold and placid,
eating its way into the muddy bank. The tethered
boats bucked a little in the breeze, complaining softly.
She understood the presence of death in the most
simple terms, as a skull and shroud moving towards
her across the grey water, a ghostly claimant from
medieval allegory. She shivered, pulling the jacket
tightly round her, conspicuously alone on the lakeside.
As the light brightened, the trees along the shore
regained their colour, the lake turned silver, an old
man shuffled along the water's edge with his hands
in his sleeves. She ran back to the cabin.

He was sitting half dressed on the edge of the bed,
watching the comics on television. His simple,
melancholy eyes stared almost unblinking at Felix
the Cat, he held a sock in one hand and her impression
was that he had been holding it for some time. She
put her arms round him and held him tightly; he
looked, over her head, at the comics. She tunnelled
her face into him, but he didn't move. She lay with
her head in his lap, listening to the bangs and screams

and crashes of Tom and Jerry in distress. Finally he got up and turned the television off, sat down in a chair and put the sock on.

'Where did you go?' It was the first question of the kind he had ever asked her; her freedom, or loneliness, diminished a little.

'Just out there, to look at the lake.'

'Is it choppy?'

'No. It's quite calm.'

She understood, now, how frightened he was. She understood how desperately hard he was trying to deal with this fear, or conceal it. . . . 'You know, while you were away a friend lent me his new Honda–450, it runs at about 7500 to 8000 revs, quite a machine, the fourth gear clicks in between sixty and seventy. It was terribly cold here—was it cold with you?—but he gave me a black oilcloth suit and a helmet and I went on the track and hit a ton. Actually I only confessed to 80 mph, not to worry him. And do you know I couldn't be frightened. I tried again next morning, same thing. Concentration, concern, care— but no fear. I don't know what to make of it. I'd imagined that past seventy I would be shaking . . .' And she had asked, misunderstanding, 'Why did you want to be frightened?' instead of realising that this was a way of dealing with extreme fear, of trying to endure death until it became familiar and comprehensible.

'Do you really have to take your boat in today?'

'Yes.'

'Why?'

'The second weekend in October is the last time.

After that everyone goes away for the winter. I've already left it late.'

'Is it far from here?'

'About twenty miles.'

'Will they all be there—the people you told me about?'

'Most of them, yes.'

She was silent, troubled for him. He went into the bathroom and said to her from there, where he couldn't be seen, 'It's all right. The first day out, afterwards, was hell. It's all right now.' He came back drying his face. 'It hurts . . . like a stump. In the same way perhaps as it hurts you. You understand?'

'Yes.'

'One lives with it.'

'Yes.'

'Get ready, then. We're off.'

His mood was remote, almost brusque. She was glad to find how little she relied on him for her happiness; he moved in and out of it like a guest with his own concerns. He put his arm round her, closed the frosted-glass door, hurried her to the car. As on the first day at the restaurant, she looked back, taking in every detail, deliberately adding this place to her memory.

*   *   *

They came to the bay down a bumpy track which Robert negotiated with great regard for the car. A dozen or so wooden and glass houses were scattered over a small hill, a grass terrace running in front of them above the water: thirty feet above the water. There was a large boathouse with a group of people standing in front of it. Robert parked the car, got out of it without waiting for her, and ran towards the group. They all turned and waved, welcoming him. She saw him go into the boathouse with three or four men.

For the first time since yesterday afternoon she felt a lurch of dismay. Women in jeans and sweaters were clustered round the boathouse door, children running about. She felt the hard brassière in her pocket and had a moment's terror because she had not put it on. I prefer myself as I am, I don't need protection, I prefer myself as I am. Slowly, she got out of the car and walked towards them, her hands in the pockets of the jacket, pulling it taut round her. As she came near them she had an overpowering impression of their health and strength, as though they were a primitive tribe living in a state of grace: their skin glowed, their hair shone, when she came up to them their eyes were bright with curiosity and goodwill.

'Hi. Did you come down with Robert?'

She thought, foolishly, that they had all known Eleanor. 'Yes. Yes, I did.'

'We didn't know if he was coming down, so we brought his boat in, but the mast's broken. I'm Julie Hemmings. This is Sue Massingham . . . Janie Eysen . . . Betty Rawlings . . .'

She smiled at them each in turn. 'Hullo . . . I'm Muriel Rowbridge.'

Robert came out of the boathouse with the men. He had taken off his shoes and socks and rolled up his

[195]

trouser legs. He did not look at her, but picked up a small, skinny child and hoisted him on to his shoulders, then started down the road to the shore, the men following. The women and the rest of the children fell in behind, the children barefoot, the women easy in their rope soles and sneakers. There was a cold wind, it was beginning to rain. She looked across the lake and saw Seal and Blair Islands, but did not know which was which. Nobody thought of telling her where they were going, or why, she was simply incorporated into the procession as though she were a passer-by.

Down by the lake there was a large, cumbersome blue boat lying almost on its side in the shallow water. The men waded round it, examining it, giving it great shoves which did not budge it at all. Somebody brought a tractor and a wagon.

'I guess we can each lift around a hundred and fifty pounds,' one man said, looking shrewdly round the group. The children were pushing at the great thing with all their might, the rain was pouring by now, the women hugged themselves, the rain soaking into their hair. Two of them were detailed to carry the mast away, they plodded staunchly up the beach against the wind, a thousand years old in their toughness and obedience. She thought momentarily, with pleasure, of the General lifting a hundred and fifty pounds, her flimsy legs pounded by water, her sparrow shoulders cracking against the bulk of the boat.

'Can I help?'

'We'll have to wait till we're told,' Julie said. 'Are you freezing?'

She was. 'No, not at all.'

'It's a dreadful old boat, home-made. Do you know it's got a bit of railway track for a keel? I can't steer it, it's far too heavy.'

'Who does it belong to?'

'An old senator, lives up the hill. He's probably still in bed.'

She didn't ask why they were taking the responsibility of bringing the senator's boat in. It was obvious that the boat, ugly and cumbersome as it was, couldn't be left to rot through the winter. Robert drove the tractor down to the water's edge, they all kicked their shoes off and rolled up their trousers and waded in, heaving at the word of command; the great hulk moved a few inches, they heaved again, panting and straining, the rain plastering the hair to their heads. At last it was near enough to be attached to the tractor and was dragged out of the water and along the beach like a dead whale. They came stamping on to the shore, shivering and laughing. She found herself piled into an estate car with the women and some of the children, driving away. Robert had not spoken to her or looked at her since they arrived. She thought that this was something to do with being a man with his friends, the custom of the tribe, some archaic need to appear strong and independent. Crouched in the back of the car, jammed between bony children, she looked at the serene wives, drenched and wind-blown but without a line on their faces, their bodies compact and well exercised, their children near at hand, and she wished that she could be like them.

Until mid-afternoon she went with the women

[197]

from house to house; they had coffee here, whisky there, helped each other out, scoured refrigerators, tied up tents and paddles, fed each other's children. Janie Eysen brought a baby and a bottle and gave them both to Muriel—'Would you mind giving her this?'

She was terrified. 'I . . . don't know how.'

'Oh, for Pete's sake, just jam it into her. When she's sick use this.' She draped a towel over Muriel's shoulder and went off somewhere. The baby nosed about blindly for the bottle, found the teat and clamped to it like a magnet. The strength and rhythm of its sucking went from her hand to her arm to her whole body. Its feet were curled, sole to sole, and its splayed hands grabbed the bottle to push it in deeper. She was astonished by the sense of achievement she felt when the baby pushed the bottle away and lay placidly squinting at her. She knew that she should now hit it for some reason, but it seemed so trusting and she felt so kindly towards it that she hoped this was unnecessary. She found herself wishing that Robert could see her with the baby; she got up, with extreme caution, and carried the baby to the window, to see if she could see him coming. She saw nothing but the rain and the squally lake, the waves like liquid steel heaving and cutting, and suddenly she knew for herself all the fear these women must have felt as they watched their husbands that day, setting out and coming back, trying to borrow boats that wouldn't sail, the two red life-jackets appearing and disappearing between the waves, the sense of helplessness.

She missed Robert as though he had been gone for

weeks instead of a few hours. There was something about the whole atmosphere of the place that made her kind of isolation, a woman by herself, the mistress or would-be mistress of other people's husbands, an anachronism. I prefer myself as I am gave way, for a moment, to I prefer myself as I could be. The baby scrabbled at her breast, burying its face in her armpit. She moved it over on to her right arm where, its head against the hard, concave chest, it seemed contented.

About three o'clock they took coffee and somebody's five-gallon bottle of whisky, the baby and the children, to Julie Hemmings' house at the top of the hill. The men began to arrive in twos and threes: tanned, substantial, quiet-spoken, they stood together at one end of the large room discussing business, machinery, sailing, property prices. The women sat on the huge sofas and drank, and discussed children, schools, the New Math, the advisability of joining health clubs during the winter months. Once they knew Muriel was not married they gave up trying to include her in the conversation, although they smiled at her a good deal and offered her more of everything than they offered each other. Each time the door opened, letting in some stranger and a gust of rain, she looked for Robert. She began to have the irrational idea that he had become disgusted with her, and had gone off in the Ferrari, leaving her here. She tried to remember whether all the men she had seen at the beach had arrived yet—they looked so alike that she couldn't be sure. The whisky, without food, had made her feel light-headed, as though she were floating on the periphery of the group of women, invisible again. They were now discussing their operations, all of which were minor and obstetrical. She could not imagine any kind of malformation or physical misfortune happening to such efficient, glossy bodies, and wondered whether she would gain their sympathy with her own, deciding that to tell them would be more of a cruelty to them than a relief to herself. She felt sure that none of them had noticed; if she had been abnormally large, Marty's chick, their eyes would have been pinned to her breast like badges.

He arrived at last. He had been dismantling an engine with Brian Stevens and they had run into some sort of trouble. Even now he didn't acknowledge her, but drank with the men at the far end of the room. One of the men went and sat, like a neutral, between the men and the women; his three-year-old son came and leant against his legs; the father began to caress the boy, stroking his bristly hair, giving him little kisses up and down his face. They were detached, father and child, in an exhausted peace of their own. Everyone spoke very quietly, the children fell asleep in corners, Julie went off to open some tins of corned-beef hash. As though he had been waiting for some signal, Robert came up to her: 'Shall we go?'

She stood up obediently. The room rocked a little.

'Go?' Julie said. 'You can't go, I'm just making some hash. Where are you going?'

'We'll go to the house,' Robert said.

'Oh come on, you can't take Muriel to the house in this weather.' There was an odd note in her voice, Muriel thought, of more than usual concern. 'We'll all be gone in a couple of hours. Stay and have some hash.'

'I think we'll go,' Robert said.

'You'll get drowned,' she said to Muriel. Muriel looked quickly at Robert. 'What are you going to eat, anyway?'

'I've got steak,' Robert said. 'We'll be all right.

She had the impression that the room was even quieter than it had been before; that everyone was listening to them and yet minding their own business.

'Are you ready?'

'Yes, of course.'

'Well, come back,' Julie said, 'if you can't make it.

'See you in April . . .'

'See you next year . . .'

'See you . . .'

They set off through the rain. He was still barefoot, carrying his shoes slung over his shoulder with a haversack. They went down the track to the beach and he led the way across the stones and boulders to the scrubby bank where trees and undergrowth grew down to the water's edge. The wind blew the rain in their faces, the waves broke against the rocks, they had to pull their way along by branches and brushwood. She took her shoes off and looked only at her feet, testing each jump and foothold, her hair slapped across her eyes, blinding her. She had to balance while she pushed it away, then slipped, clinging to a branch just in time. At last he waited for her. She shouted against the wind, 'This is meant to be a joke: Do you always kill your girl-friends?' After a moment he grinned widely and took her hand, but it was more

[201]

difficult holding him and she let him go on, surefooted, while she scrambled behind him, her stockings shredded, feet bleeding. At last there was a slippery path going straight up from the rocks to a small shack entirely enclosed by trees and water. He opened the door and she stumbled in, falling down on the bed exhausted. As she lay there on her stomach she heard him moving about busily, the crack of dry wood as it caught fire. When she rolled on to her back the fire was roaring, he was standing over her with a pair of jeans and a shirt in his hand.

'You'd better put these on. The steak won't be long.'

He went away behind a partition, the hiss and smell of frying steak. She changed, and hung her clothes by the fire. She had felt curiously diffident and uneasy with him all day and now, although all the ingredients for happiness were there, she felt that something had to be made clear before she could go on. Perhaps, after all, he couldn't stand the sight of her one-sided body; perhaps seeing her among his friends, Eleanor's friends, had made him realise how foreign she was, or how little they knew about each other. Certainly he was entirely different from the neat, urban lawyer she had met a week ago; there was a kind of strength about him, a madness she didn't understand. She wanted to talk to him this evening, not to make love until they had talked.

'Come and eat. Are you really exhausted?' He was tender again.

'No. I'm well. And you?'

'I'm well.'

They sat at a wooden table and ate the soft, almost

[202]

raw, peppery steak with one knife. It was dark now outside, the hut shaken by the rain and wind, he lit an oil lamp and their shadows wavered gargantuan on the wall.

'Romantic?' he asked.

'Very.'

'You think we're really in a movie, or a novel?'

'No.'

'Neither do I. I spend a lot of time here in the summer. By myself. In good weather it's not at all romantic. I read, sail, cook, lie about. There are squirrels in the wood, kyotes, even bears. In the evening I go over to the harbour and come back drunk.'

'The way we came? Or in the boat?'

'In the boat. There's something great about rowing through black water when you're drunk. Ulysses knew it. What we find romantic now is . . . the sense of danger.'

'I don't feel in danger. I feel very safe. It's silent. Warm. It's never going to end.' She had moved on again after the block, she was proceeding smoothly. 'I'm happy.'

'But it is going to end, you know that.'

'Perhaps in a way it won't.'

He poured more wine and leant back, tipping his chair so that his face was in shadow. 'Tell me something. What will you do on Wednesday when you get home?'

The question surprised her. They had not mentioned her going home since he had rung the airline yesterday. Apart from her vague, ecstatic vision of freedom and

[203]

writing something, she had not thought about it. She said, 'I don't know. I'll . . . go to the flat.'

'Will anybody be there?'

'Ramsey is there. I must tell him I'm coming back.

'I thought that was over.'

'It is. That's why I must tell him, so that he can go. He doesn't know where to go, unless it's to his wife, or me.'

'So he'll go back to his wife?'

'No. I don't think she wants him.'

'That's sad. Do you want him?'

'He won't be there. I'll . . . oh, I don't know, unpack, see what's happened. I suppose I'll ring the General.' She was doing all these things as she described them. It was cruel.

'The one who warned you about the martinis? And what will she say?'

'Well . . . she'll say come back to work on Thursday. She'll ask me if I had a good time. She'll tell me the gossip.'

'So on Thursday you'll make up your face and put on your little journalist's suit, and that breastplate again, and you'll go to work on the subway . . .'

'The bus.'

'You'll go to work on the bus. And when will you write something?'

'I don't know.'

'Who will love you? This Ramsey?'

'I don't know.'

He banged the chair forward, rocketing back into the light. 'So what happened in the car yesterday wasn't really anything? You leaned forward like a rider approaching a bank-and-fence, you leaned forward and collected with a smile showing on the side from within, and you said "Something's happened", and I said I knew, and you said, "I'm going to write something". And to tell you the truth this moment sounded so . . . precious that I couldn't talk or even look, I don't know if I took your hand, it was as if you were going to be hurt, if I took your hand it was the way you hold a child to put alcohol on a cut. And all that means nothing?'

'No. It meant something. I've never been so happy.'

'Happy!' He spat the word out, disgusted. 'Is that all you want, to say I was so happy?'

'I can't go back and just . . . write. Write in a vacuum. I've got to make money . . .'

'So? Writing doesn't make money?'

'Maybe not. I mean, I will write something. I'm going to. But I can't just give up my job . . .'

He interrupted her. 'You want some coffee?'

'No, thank you.' She was distressed, as anyone is distressed who hears the truth and doesn't know what to do about it. She watched him as he took the plates away, put more wood on the fire.

'What's the alternative?' she asked. 'There isn't one.'

He stood with his back to her, looking down at the fire. 'You can stay.'

'Here?'

'In the summer you could stay here.'

'I don't understand. How could I stay here?'

He squatted down and poked the fire with a long branch. It caught light and he threw it on the fire. 'You could marry me.'

[205]

'*Marry* you?'

He swivelled round on his heels and sat easily on
them. 'I tell you. This morning I woke up and you
weren't there. I wanted you to be there. Most of my
friends are married, but I don't know anything about
it. Don't understand it, if you like. I just knew that
I wanted you to be there every day, as far as I could
see. I suppose that means marriage.'

She began to say something, but he went on quickly,
'That's not all. I thought about it all day. It would be
good for you, you would be free, you could write,
you wouldn't be bugged by this . . . General, this
Ramsey. And we could have children.'

'Children?'

'Sure. Children. Why not? Wouldn't you like
that?'

'Yes, but . . .'

'I can support you, if that's what you're worrying
about.'

'Of course it isn't. Of course it isn't.'

'I suppose I should give you time to think about it,
or something. But there isn't any time.'

'You mean you would want me to stay tomorrow?'

'Of course. We could go over to England later—
Christmas, maybe.'

She was inexpressibly moved. All the things that
flooded into her mind could not, for the moment, be
said. They were all irrelevant. She got up and walked
across the room, holding on to the iron rail of the
bedstead, feeling it cold and gritty in her clenched
hands.

'*Marry* you?'

[206]

'Is it such a very extraordinary idea?'

'Yes. No. Of course it's not an extraordinary idea.'

'It seems very simple to me.'

'Do you . . . love me, then?'

'Isn't that what I'm saying?'

'I don't know.'

He got up and came over to her, putting his arms all the way round her, enveloping her. 'We will get married,' he said. 'It makes sense.'

She pushed him away gently and went and sat on the table, her feet propped on one of the stools, her hands shielding her face from the fire and from his sight. She couldn't bear him to see how grateful she was. If she could have said I love you, hurray, I want you, of course, without this overwhelming gratitude, it would have seemed simple to her too. She had to try to make him understand, and she didn't want to.

He came and sat on the other stool. 'Are we going to talk about it?'

'Shouldn't we?'

'If you're going to say that it's because I'm sorry for you, don't. It would be insulting and untrue. I want you as you are. I never knew you before, so as far as I'm concerned you have always been as you are. You understand?'

'Supposing . . . it happens again?'

'Then it happens again. You're still better off with me.'

'But what about you?'

'I can look after myself. I always have done.'

'But'—she threw her hands out, almost as though

[207]

she were exasperated—'you give me all this. What do I give you back? Trouble.'

'All I give you in that way is security. It's what men are meant to give women, I believe. I don't want to be conventional. I just have it to give you, that's all. What good is it to me?'

'But . . .'

He caught her hand as though he were catching a flying ball. 'Look, if you don't want to marry me, forget it. There's no point in arguing about it.'

'But I have to say what I think.'

'Of course. I'm sorry. Say what you think.'

She slipped off the table and went to the bed again, to be away from him. What did she think? That she had been happier with him than at any other time she could remember. That he had brought her to life again. That the future he was offering was valuable and real, in contrast to the future by herself, which was unknown and terrifying. That if gratitude and happiness were a form of love, she loved him. She knew now that the sense of mourning, the feeling that all this was coming from the wrong person, was futile. At last there was a direct path through the wilderness, away from the barrier, away from isolation. Away from home? Well, it was time.

On the other hand . . . But the other hand was empty. She only had to say yes, and the decision would be made.

'I don't know. I don't know.'

'Then don't worry. I'm sorry if I seemed to be rushing you. Think about it as long as you like. I'm probably wrong to want to keep you tomorrow.'

'No, you're not, you're not.' She was already denying him, giving him nothing back, feeling unable to respond to his generosity. She ran to him across the room, held him, blinding herself against his chest. He pushed her head back and looked at her face.

'All right,' she said.

'You mean it?'

'Yes, I mean it.'

She had never given anyone so much before. He lifted her up, lifted her off her feet. He was laughing or crying, holding her like a prize he must show off to the entire world. She clung to him for safety, laughing with him, drunk with his sense of relief. I've cheated him, I've lied to him. You haven't, stop it, stop thinking, it's true. She shut her eyes tightly, kissing him again and again, proving herself through her mouth and lips and tongue, as though she would enter him and, being part of him, have no more problems. He carried her to the bed and they made love as though completing a capture, fighting with teeth and nails to subdue each other, using all their strength.

*   *   *

Before they slept he put huge logs on the fire and made her wear an old, scratchy, schoolboy dressing gown. He said he would give up his apartment and buy a house, she needed a room to work in, they would have a maid. He said that if the shack was too primitive he would get one of the houses on the harbour, where she would have friends, but she said no, she liked the shack. He said he would teach her to sail.

'Would you have married Eleanor if . . . ?'

'Yes.' After a long silence he asked, 'Would you have married Ramsey?'

'Yes. Yes, I think so.'

The mention of these two names made a distance between them. He felt this, and held her closely, but they both dreamed of the past and, when they woke in the night, did not tell each other.

16

THERE were a lot of things to be done. She had only brought clothes for a week, he said they could buy enough to keep her going until she could get some made. She imagined herself going back to Yves Pretin and, sitting idly on a small golden chair, ordering an entire wardrobe. She had to tell the General. He asked her if she thought the General would be upset, and she answered truthfully that the General would be delighted. She said that she would like to telephone Ramsey and tell him that he could stay in the flat. He said that from the sound of Ramsey he would probably stay there anyway, and again there was a short silence between them, a distance. He promised that they would go over to London in a month or so to see her parents and pack up her possessions. She knew that apart from her notebooks she didn't need any of her possessions; as for her parents, her mother would be thankful and her father was blind. It was all very easy. Too easy? The fire had gone out by morning, and he didn't light it again. She was cold all through, and her happiness had a feeling of unreality, as though she were slightly drugged.

She wanted to tidy the place up, but he wouldn't

let her. He was insistent that she left the bed unmade and that she wore one of his sweaters, leaving her own there. It was as though he too might want to prove, in the future, that the night had been real. When he had locked the door he tied the key to a piece of holly and hid it under the steps. She thought now I know where the key is, I know the way in, and this seemed an added confirmation, a symbol of no longer being shut out. The rain had stopped, the sun was shining, the way back seemed easy.

He said, 'Let's go and see if Brian's still here. He's my greatest friend, I'd like him to meet you.'

'Will you tell him . . . about us?'

'Not if you don't want me to.'

'I'd sooner we kept it to ourselves, for now.'

'Why?'

She laughed. 'He might not like me.'

'He'll like you all right.'

'He's the one who . . . rescued you that day.'

'Yes. But we don't talk about it.'

There seemed many things that were not talked about; many compartments to be kept closed. The houses of the people who would soon be her friends were locked and shuttered, a few old toys lying about in the scrubby grass, a rubber sandal on the beach. Brian Stevens was loading up his car—a quiet, sandy man with rimless spectacles over pale blue eyes. He and Robert touched each other's shoulders for a moment with the flats of their hands, Robert introduced her and then they stood peacefully for a while, looking out across the lake.

'Docked the *Triumph*?'

'Couple of weeks back.'

'Mike's fixing your mast.'

'Yes.'

'Came down in the Ferrari, did you?'

'Yes.'

'How long did it take?'

'We stopped overnight.'

'Ah.' He turned the pale blue, knowledgeable eyes on Muriel. 'How do you like it over here, Miss Rowbridge?'

'Very much.'

'Staying long?'

'I . . .'

'I hope so,' Robert said.

Brian nodded. 'Well, then. Better get moving. You all packed up?'

'I don't bother.'

'No. Well. Be seeing you, then.'

'Be seeing you, Brian. Take care now.'

It hardly seemed the conversation of great friends, but she knew she had a lot to learn.

'He liked you,' Robert said, as they walked towards the car.

'How can you tell?' she asked dryly.

'I've got a lot of different sides to my life. This is one of them. The office, my friends at home, they're something else.'

'And which side of your life do you like best?'

'I don't know,' he said gravely. 'I suppose the side I spend alone, just reading, playing records. Thinking.'

'Your bachelor life,' she said, smiling over the words.

'Not necessarily. Even a married man can read.' He kissed her, and shut her into the car. They were both tired, and didn't talk very much on the way back.

*　　　*　　　*

She had not written anything in the notebook since her scribbled warning to herself in the hotel, before meeting MacNeish. The romantic fever of the previous week, now tempered to a small, private sadness, had driven her into a kind of delirium in which writing had been a gathering together of her life into a bright, untidy gift. The gift had been over-looked, it was still her own and she had realised that she could use it for herself. It had made her feel rich and powerful, as though she carried magic in her head. Now she thought about marriage to Robert, the end of loneliness and uncertainty, and she didn't want to write about it. She didn't want to write about anything. The adult world, in which things are what they seem and the eyes look outward, had become a reality at last. Childlike make-believe, pretending to be a strange creature living in a wilderness, running after antique shapes and shadows, flying by night, picking over bones and shells and flowers, changing rooms into deserts through which she travelled at her last gasp—all this, she knew, was almost over. The scorpion would reach the other side of the river, shake hands with the frog and continue on its way, practising survival. If she wrote anything, it would be fiction based on the implausible behaviour of survivors, there would be no unanswerable 'Why?', no death beckoning her from the water; everything would have a purpose and, if she died, she would survive in Robert. Survive, perhaps, in her children. But she would not have children, not until she knew that she was going to live.

She would have to tell him this. In five years, when she was certain; but not now. He wanted, she knew, to take children to the lake, to carry his own son on his shoulders—she could see the son, hair shaggy on the nape of his neck, different, absorbed with the shapes of stones and light on the water. He was a child of her imagination, she would not give him a dead mother.

She looked at Robert driving, and put her hand over his on the wheel. He turned and smiled at her; the smile was sad, as though he could hear her thoughts. We'll have a complete check-up, he was saying, you'll see there's not the slightest danger, you're going to live to be ninety. It's not good enough, she said. You must wait.

'There's no point in waiting,' he said. 'Let's get a special licence, do it right away.'

'Isn't it complicated, being English?'

'I don't see why.'

*   *   *

It was late afternoon by the time they reached the city, traffic thick on the freeways, lines of patient cars queuing at every stop-light. She began to feel absurdly anxious, as though she were going to catch the plane after all; but she imagined that this anxiety was about

[215]

ringing up the airline and cancelling her reservation in time. He began his snatches of tuneless song, as he always did in heavy traffic, perhaps out of nervousness. He was again the Robert of the first night, courteous, tight-lipped, with the decorousness of a foreigner. Ta-rum-ta-ra-rum, tarum, tarum—the 'Blue Danube'. She wondered suddenly what he had been doing at those two receptions, neatly suited and white collared; she remembered the wives with their modestly covered knees, twenty-one pearls strung round each ageing neck. She had never been to Cheltenham, but that was the name that came to her mind: eternal Cheltenham.

'How old are you, Robert?'

'Thirty-six. Too old for you?'

'No, of course not. I thought . . . you were older.'

'I shall soon be bald. Will you mind?'

She smiled, but didn't say anything. Ta-rum, ta-rum, ta-rum, ta-rum—'Tales from the Vienna Woods'. She realised that she was digging her nails into the palms of her hands, and relaxed her hands deliberately, making them lie open on her lap.

'Church or register office?' he asked.

She answered, unthinking, 'Oh, register office.'

'All right.'

He was, perhaps, making lists in his head; the items in the lists marched in on her like marching railings, the gate would be the last to be fixed and padlocked.

She asked, 'Do you believe . . . in being faithful?'

'Of course. Don't you?'

'Yes. Yes, I do, but . . . I just wonder if it's possible. I mean for all those years.'

'It is if you want it to be possible. If you don't there's not much point.'

'Are you jealous?'

'Not particularly, no. I've never had any reason to be.'

He answered her questions calmly, with complete certainty. It seemed that he thought she had a right to cross-question him. He did not, however, ask her the same questions; his 'Don't you?' was a confirmation of his own attitude, she could not possibly have answered, 'No.'

'I haven't told you anything about me,' she said, beginning to struggle.

'All the important things.'

'But there might be important things I haven't told you.'

'I don't think so.'

Their only shared experience from the past had been the prospect, at moments it had seemed to both of them the probability, of death. She saw a piece of paper that Ramsey had pinned up in front of her typewriter at home; she saw the blue felt-pen writing, the two brass drawing pins: 'Art has two constant, two unending concerns: it always meditates on death and thus always creates life. All great, genuine art resembles and continues the Revelation of St. John.' She saw this so clearly that she could read the words, rather than remember them.

'Why did you put that up?' she had asked him.

'To comfort you. Maybe to get you going.'

That had been while she was writing the beauty column. She had not taken it down afterwards. It would still be there, although perhaps the bottom edge had curled up in the sun. Ten days, a lifetime ago, it had been there.

'What terrible traffic,' she said.

'Yes,' he said. 'It's the rush hour.'

*   *   *

The flat had been cleaned and tidied, her clothes folded neatly on top of her suitcase, the single bed reverted to a sofa with hard, tasselled head cushions. The blinds were down, the heating high. She took the brassière out of his jacket pocket and put it into the suitcase, since there was nowhere else. Then she hung the jacket neatly in the cupboard. He was hastily leafing through his mail.

'Shall I ring the airline for you?' he asked.

'No. No, it's all right, I'll do it.'

'You want to call London?'

'Maybe. Yes. Later.'

He came and held her tightly. She said, without knowing exactly what she meant, 'Thank you. Thank you.'

'For what?'

'I don't know. Everything. The night, the place, the . . . steak. The Fascination Room. Asking me to marry you. The man on the ferry.'

'What did he say?'

' "Have a good time, whatever your endeavour may be." '

He stroked her hair. They were close, and very still. When he spoke his voice was oddly rasping.

'I'm going to have a shower. I'll leave you to your telephoning.'

'All right.' She felt as though she were being left to say goodbye to a corpse, something you do more decently in private.

'Fix yourself a drink if you want one.'

'Yes. All right. Thank you.'

She waited while he found a clean shirt and went into the bathroom, slamming the door. Then, slowly, she approached the telephone.

'Can I help you?'

'Yes. I . . . my name's Muriel Rowbridge. I have a reservation on Flight 101 to London this evening. I think it's Flight 101.'

'Flight 101 is correct. You wish to confirm your reservation, Miss Rowbridge?'

'No. I want to . . . I . . .' She was wringing the receiver as though it were a third, anguished hand. 'What time does the flight leave?'

'Eight-forty-five,' the voice said patiently. 'Check in no later than seven-thirty.'

'How late can I cancel it?'

'If you're going to cancel it, Miss Rowbridge, I suggest that you do that now. It's already six-fifteen.'

'But I don't know . . . I can't tell . . .' The last forty-eight hours were streaming through her mind, she wanted to catch them and keep them, but they were away in a golden dust-cloud, speeding away from her into never, never more, never again . . . She was left holding a telephone in a strange, hot room, about to take a decision that would alter her life.

'Are you there?' the voice said more tartly.

'Yes. Yes, I am.'

'Now do you wish to confirm or cancel this reservation?'

'I want to confirm it,' she said.

★   ★   ★

'Ramsey?'

'Good God! Where on earth are you?'

'Ramsey, I'm coming back tonight.'

'Are you all right? Is everything . . . all right?'

'Yes. It's just . . . the distance. Are you all right?'

'Yes, I'm all right, I'm fine. You'll want me to go, then.'

'Will you come and meet me?'

'I'm sorry. I can't hear. Will I what?'

'Come and meet me. The plane gets in at six-forty-five. Will you come, Ramsey?'

There was a long silence. The waves sighed over the telephone cables, fish brushed against them with their silver bodies.

'Yes,' he said. 'I'll be there.'

She put down the receiver and covered her face with her hands. Her hands were drenched with tears. She did not realise that she had been crying. When she heard him come in from the bathroom, she couldn't move. He seemed to stand motionless for a long time. Then he said quietly, 'You're going.'

'Yes. Yes, I'm going.'

'I knew,' he said, 'that you would be going.'

★   ★   ★

At some point during the next half-hour, which seemed a moment stretched into unendurable time, the telephone rang.

'It's for you,' he said, handing her the receiver.

'For me? From England?'

'No.'

She didn't know anyone else. Her face was puffy and sticky like a child's.

'Muriel? Hi, there. Ready for your lift to the airport?' It was a ghost voice, rich and caressing and full of unspoken worries.

'Alex. No. I'm sorry. I forgot. I can't. I . . .'

'You mean you're staying on? That's good news.'

'No, I'm not staying. I'm going. But someone else is taking me.'

'You mean you've been unfaithful to me already? Oh come on. Stand him up. I've got the whole thing organised.'

She didn't think she would get to the end of the sentence: 'No, Alex, I'm sorry, I'll see you in London, ring me . . .' She rang off. It seemed the most irrelevant conversation of her whole life. She could not clearly remember what Alex MacNeish looked like. He had been a dream that she had written down; she would remember him only when she read the dream. Robert had gone into the other room while she had been talking and she could not call him back. This was the beginning, perhaps the most painful time of their parting.

However, he couldn't keep away. He covered his suffering with a thin briskness, a hopeless attempt to be jolly. They longed to touch each other, but kept far apart in the small room, he sitting in the armchair with his knees drawn in, she scooping and bundling her clothes, forcing them into the bulging suitcase. She had left the brassière out, and began closing the suitcase. He got up, took the brassière; she stood aside, he opened the suitcase, put the brassière in, closed the case and snapped the locks.

'Don't wear it,' he said. 'Go as you are.'

She gave in, clinging to him as though she were drowning; but after a moment he detached himself and made her stand alone. He was crying.

★   ★   ★

In the dark, anonymous bar at the airport they sat like distant acquaintances, asking no questions, revealing nothing, not speaking of the future or the past.

'Why are the bars so dark?'

'So that people can't see each other.'

'I wonder why they like not seeing each other.'

'I don't know. Perhaps because it's easier to tell lies.'

'I suppose it's mostly business men who go to bars.'

'That's right. They have to tell a lot of lies. They keep their hats on, too. This makes them unrecognisable in the outside world.'

'Announcing the departure of Flight 101 for London. Will all passengers proceed to Gate 37 and have their boarding passes ready ... Announcing the departure of Flight 101 ...'

He said, 'My bones are clenched.'

'I can't go.'

'Yes, you can. I'm not coming with you. Please go.'

'I shall write to you.'

'Yes.'

'Why am I going? Why? Why am I going?'

He smiled very faintly and at last took her hand, holding it so tightly that she felt the bones would break. 'Because,' he said, 'it is your nature.'

She reached for her suitcase. 'Will you stay here?'

'Yes.'

'Goodbye, Robert.'

'Goodbye.'

She got up and walked to the door. She didn't want to look back, but found her head turning, her body turning, as though even now she might return to him. He was holding a coaster in both hands, the small piece of cardboard like a sheet of iron which he might tear apart. She walked through the door, leaving him.

*   *   *

The stewardess was demonstrating the use of a life-jacket. She touched the lungs, the nipples of the jacket with delicate fingers, no more than indicating the nozzle and tapes. Her hands moved swiftly, lightly, through gestures which, in the real event, would be terrified and clumsy. The stewardess smiled all the time, her eyes were smiling as her fingers hovered, brushed against her yellow breasts.

The young woman sat with a notebook in her lap, a ball-point pen clipped to its cover. Her eyes were full of tears, and yet there was an expression on her face that was not entirely sad; the expression, perhaps, of someone who has just been moved by a sad and true story which they will never entirely forget. After a little while, the tears still wet on her cheeks, she unclipped the pen, opened the notebook and began to write.